ピアス

Snakes and Earrings

Translated from the Japanese by
David James Karashima

Originally published in Japanese
as *Hebi ni piasu*

DUTTON

Hitomi Kanehara

Snakes

and

Earrings

DUTTON
Published by Penguin Group (USA) Inc.
375 Hudson Street, New York, New York 10014, U.S.A.
Penguin Group (Canada), 10 Alcorn Avenue, Toronto, Ontario, Canada M4V 3B2 (a division of
Pearson Penguin Canada Inc.); Penguin Books Ltd, 80 Strand, London WC2R 0RL, England; Pen-
guin Ireland, 25 St Stephen's Green, Dublin 2, Ireland (a division of Penguin Books Ltd); Penguin
Group (Australia), 250 Camberwell Road, Camberwell, Victoria 3124, Australia (a division of Pear-
son Australia Group Pty Ltd); Penguin Books India Pvt Ltd, 11 Community Centre, Panchsheel
Park, New Delhi – 110 017, India; Penguin Books (NZ), cnr Airborne and Rosedale Roads, Albany,
Auckland 1310, New Zealand (a division of Pearson New Zealand Ltd); Penguin Books (South
Africa) (Pty) Ltd, 24 Sturdee Avenue, Rosebank, Johannesburg 2196, South Africa

Penguin Books Ltd, Registered Offices: 80 Strand, London WC2R 0RL, England

Published by Dutton, a member of Penguin Group (USA) Inc.
Originally published in Japanese as *Hebi ni piasu* in January 2004 by Shueisha, Inc.

First printing, May 2005
1   3   5   7   9   10   8   6   4   2

Copyright © 2005 by Hitomi Kanehara
Translation © 2005 David James Karashima
All rights reserved

REGISTERED TRADEMARK—MARCA REGISTRADA

LIBRARY OF CONGRESS CATALOGING-IN-PUBLICATION DATA
Kanehara, Hitomi.
[Hebi ni piasu. English]
Snakes and earrings / Hitomi Kanehara.
p.   cm.
ISBN 0-525-94889-9 (alk. paper)
I. Title.

PL855.A528H4313   2005
895.6'36—dc22
2005001594

Printed in the United States of America
Set in Adobe Garamond
Designed by Katy Riegel

PUBLISHER'S NOTE
This book is a work of fiction. Names, characters, places, and incidents either are the product of the
author's imagination or are used fictitiously, and any resemblance to actual persons, living or dead,
business establishments, events, or locales is entirely coincidental.

This book is printed on acid-free paper.

Snakes and Earrings

"Know what a forked tongue is?"

"One that's split in two?"

"Yeah, like the tongue of a snake or lizard. Except sometimes . . . they don't belong to a snake, and they don't belong to a lizard."

He deliberately removed the cigarette from his lips and stuck out his tongue. Its tip was clearly split in two, just like that of a snake. Then I watched, transfixed, as he lifted the right tip of it, then skillfully grasped his cigarette in the crux of the "V."

"Whoa . . ."

This was my first encounter with a forked tongue.

"Why don't you give it a try too?" he said.

And without thought, by instinct alone, I nodded.

Getting a forked tongue is normally something done by crazy people. They call it "body modification." But that

1

didn't stop me from listening intently as he explained how it was done. Apparently, you begin by getting your tongue pierced. You then gradually enlarge the hole by inserting bigger and bigger tongue rings. Then, when the hole has been stretched to a certain size, you tie dental floss or fishing line in tight loops running from the hole down the middle of the tongue. Finally, you cut the remaining part of the tongue that's still connected using either a scalpel or a razor blade. In fact, some people don't even bother going through the whole pierce-and-tie process at all—they just slice their tongue in two with a scalpel.

"But is it safe? I mean, don't people normally die when they bite their tongue off?" I asked.

"It's safe. You cauterize the tongue to stop the bleeding. Anyway, that's just the quick method. Personally, I started with a tongue ring. It takes time, that's true, but it's worth it for a cleaner cut."

The idea of a cauterizing iron pressed against a bloody tongue made my skin crawl, though I'm no stranger to body modification of a kind.

My thing until now has been earrings. And to describe my earrings, I guess I should begin by telling you how they're measured. The thickness of body jewelry is generally measured in gauges; the lower the number, the larger the hole. Starter earrings are usually either 16g or 14g, which is about 1.5mm wide. After 0g comes 00g, which is about 9.5mm wide. Anything over a centimeter wide is measured in fractions of gauges. But to be honest, once you go over 00 you look like a member of some kind of tribe and it's no longer really a question of looking good or not. As for me, I have two 0g earrings in my right ear, and my left ear is lined with 0g, 2g, and 4g earrings from the bottom up. As you can imagine, it was painful enough stretching the holes in my ears; I couldn't begin to imagine how much it would hurt to do the same to my tongue.

I used to wear 16g earrings until I met a girl two years older than me named Eri at a club one night and I fell in love with her 00g earrings. When I told her how cool her earrings looked, she gave me dozens of her old ones, ranging from 12g to 0g, saying, "Once you go this far, you can't wear smaller ones anymore." Going from 16 to 6 was easy, but going from 4 to 2 and then 2 to 0 was a *real* stretch. Blood oozed from the hole and my earlobes became swollen and red. The constant, thumping pain lasted for two or three days. I also inherited Eri's philosophy of not using expanders, so it took me three months to get down to a 0g. I was just thinking of moving on to 00g the night I met the guy with the forked tongue. I was addicted to stretching, and I guess that fueled my interest in his talk of tongue splitting. I noticed that he seemed to be enjoying himself too.

A few days later I went with Ama the snakeman to Desire—a kind of punk/alternative store in a side-street basement just off the shopping and entertainment district. The first thing that came into sight when I walked in was a close-up shot of a vagina with a pierced vulva, and the walls were lined with photos of pierced scrotums and tattoos too. Further inside, there was a range of regular body jewelry and various accessories on display. There was also a selection of whips and cock cases. Basically, it was a store for perverts.

Ama called out and a guy popped his head out from behind the counter. He was about twenty-four or twenty-five and had a curled-up dragon tattooed on the back of his shaved head.

"Hey, Ama. Long time no see."

"Lui, this is Shiba-san. This is his store. Shiba-san, this is my girlfriend."

To be honest I didn't really consider myself Ama's girl, but I kept my mouth shut and bowed anyway.

"Ah, I see. You found yourself a cute one."

I felt slightly nervous.

"We're here to get her tongue pierced."

"Is that right? So even Barbie-girls get their tongues pierced, huh?" said Shiba-san, eyeing me curiously.

"I'm not a Barbie-girl."

"She wants a split tongue too," said Ama, laughing teasingly, as if he hadn't heard what I had said. I remembered once being told at a body jewelry store that the tongue was the most painful body part to get pierced, second only to the genitals. I was beginning to wonder whether it was a good idea to let a guy like this do it.

"Come here and let me see your tongue," said Shiba-san.

I stepped up to the counter and stuck out my tongue. Shiba-san leaned slightly forward and said, "Well, it looks pretty thin, so it shouldn't hurt too much."

I felt a slight sense of relief.

"But when you order grilled beef, isn't the tongue the toughest kind of meat after the stomach?" I asked. I had been wondering all along whether it was really safe to put a hole through such a tough part of the body.

"Good point," said Shiba-san. "Well, it'll definitely hurt more than getting your ears pierced. I mean, you're putting a hole in your tongue. That's bound to hurt."

"Don't scare her, Shiba-san. If I could do it, Lui, I don't see why you can't."

"Not to mention you fainted. Anyway, bring that tongue of yours over here."

Shiba-san pointed past the counter and smiled at me, and I noticed that he had a crooked smile. He had piercings in his eyelids, eyebrows, lips, nose, and cheeks. So much so that they hid his expression, making it almost impossible to tell what he was thinking. I also noticed that the backs of his hands were covered in keloid scars. At first I thought they might be the result of some kind of accident. But as I looked at them out of the corner of my eye, I noticed that each burn was a circle of about a centimeter wide—about the size of a cigarette end, if you know what I mean. Basically this guy was completely mad. Ama was the very first person of his type that I had gotten to know. And now there was Shiba-san, who didn't have a split tongue, but did wear a faceful of piercings that gave him an intimidating look. Ama and I followed Shiba-san into the back room. I sat down on a pipe chair that Shiba-san pointed me to and looked around the room. There was a bed, some unusual looking tools and, of course, shady photos on the walls.

"You do tattoos here too?" I asked.

"Yep. I'm a tattoo artist myself. Though I got someone else to do this one," said Shiba-san, pointing to his head.

"I got mine done here too," said Ama.

The night I met Ama, we had hit it off talking about forked tongues, and he had taken me back to his place. Ama had taken photos of the entire tongue splitting process, from stretching his tongue hole to slicing the tip in two with a scalpel. I had looked through the photos one by one. Ama had stretched his tongue hole to 00g, so he only had to cut about 5mm with the scalpel, but it still bled a surprising amount. After that, Ama had shown me an underground Web site with video footage of the tongue-splitting process. To Ama's amazement, I watched the footage over and over again. I didn't know why it excited me so much. Later on that night I slept with him. And afterward, as he showed off the dragon tattoo that stretched across his upper arm and back, I told myself that I would also get a tattoo, once my tongue was split.

"I want to get a tattoo."

"For real?" Shiba-san and Ama said at once.

"Cool. It would look great. Tattoos come out much better on women than on men. Especially young women. You can tattoo really detailed drawings on such fine skin," said Shiba-san, stroking my upper arm.

"Shiba-san. First things first. The tongue stud."

"Oh, right." Shiba-san reached forward and grabbed a piercer in a plastic bag off the steel rack. It was an ordinary piercing gun used for ears.

"Stick out your tongue. Now, where do you want the hole?"

I stuck my tongue out and pointed to a spot about two centimeters in from the very tip. With a practiced hand, Shiba-san wiped my tongue with a piece of cotton and put a black dot on the point I had indicated.

"Put your chin on the table."

I did as I was told and bent down with my tongue

still sticking out. Shiba-san placed a towel under my tongue and placed the stud in the piercer. But the moment I saw the stud, I slapped Shiba-san's arm and shook my head.

"What's the problem?"

"That's a 12g, right? You're not going to start me off with that, are you?"

"Yeah, it's a 12. I mean, you don't see people wearing 16 or 18 on their tongue, do you? It'll be fine."

"Please use a 14."

I pleaded with Ama and Shiba-san and convinced them to use a 14 instead. I always used a 14 or 16 for starter earrings. Shiba-san placed a 14g stud in the gun and said, "This is where you want it, right?"

I nodded slightly and tightened my fists. My palms were already sweaty, slimy, and uncomfortable. Shiba-san positioned the piercing gun and pushed the tip against the towel. He slowly slipped the piercer over my tongue. I could feel the cold metal stud on the back of my tongue.

"Ready?" asked Shiba-san gently. I glanced up and gave a little nod. "Here it comes," he said, and put his finger on the trigger. His words made me picture him having sex. I wondered if he warned girls of his climax with the same soft voice. The next moment there was a clamping sound, and shivers much greater than those of an orgasm shot through my entire body. Goose bumps shot up my arms, and my body went into a slight spasm. My stomach tightened and for some reason so did my crotch, where I felt an ecstatic, tingling sensation. The piercing gun snapped open, releasing the stud. Free once again, I grimaced and slipped my tongue back into my mouth.

"Let me see," said Shiba-san, turning my head toward him and sticking out his tongue.

With watery eyes I stuck out my now numb tongue.

"Looks fine. It's in straight and in the right spot."

Ama came in between us and stared at my tongue.

"You're right. Good for you, Lui," said Ama.

My tongue was burning and I found it difficult even to speak.

"Lui, right?" said Shiba-san. "You sure can take pain. I hear that girls have more tolerance for pain than guys. Some people faint when they get sensitive parts like the tongue and genitals pierced."

I nodded and indicated without opening my mouth that I understood. Dull and sharp pains hit me in short waves. I was glad I had listened to Ama and come here. If I had tried doing it myself as I had initially planned, I probably would have given up halfway. I was given some ice for my tongue, and I could feel the excitement gradually drain away. Once I had calmed down, Ama and I browsed through the body jewelry in the store. Ama got tired of looking at the body jewelry and walked over to the corner where the S&M goods were on display. I found Shiba-san, who had come out of the back room, and leaned against the counter.

"What do you think of forked tongues?" I asked.

Shiba-san shrugged and said, "I think it's an interesting idea, but unlike piercings and tattoos, it involves actually changing the shape of the body. I wouldn't want to do that myself. I think only God has the right to do that."

For some reason his words were very convincing, and I gave a big nod. I tried to think of all the different types of body modification I knew of. There was foot-binding, waist-tightening with a corset, and neck-extension practiced by some tribes. I wondered whether or not braces counted.

"If you were God, what kind of human would you create?" I asked.

"I wouldn't change how they look. But I would make them as dumb as chickens. So dumb they'd never even imagine the existence of a god."

I looked up slightly at Shiba-san. He'd said the words nonchalantly, but his eyes were laughing with mischief. This guy, I thought, was bizarre.

"Can you show me some tattoo designs sometime?" I asked.

"Sure," said Shiba-san with a smile, his eyes filled with kindness. His eyes were unnaturally brown and his skin was white. Almost as white as a Caucasian.

"Give me a call anytime. Even if it's just to ask a question about your tongue stud." Shiba-san wrote his cell phone number on the back of the store's business card and handed it to me. I took it and thanked him. I shot a glance toward Ama, who was examining a whip that he had picked up, and slipped the card into my wallet, the sight of which reminded me that I hadn't paid.

"I should pay," I said. "How much is it?"

"Don't worry about it," said Shiba-san as if he couldn't care less.

I put my elbows on the counter, rested my face in my hands and watched him. He was perched on a stool on the other side of the counter. He seemed to find it annoying that I was looking at him and he tried not to meet my eyes. Without looking at me, he said in a deliberate tone, "Looking at your face gets the sadist in me all revved up."

"Well, I'm a masochist, so perhaps I'm giving off that kind of vibe," I said.

Shiba-san stood up and finally looked me in my eyes with great tenderness, as if he were looking at a puppy. He leaned forward to bring his eyes level to mine, pushed up my chin with his thin fingers, and smiled.

"I'd just love to stab this neck with a needle," he said, looking as if he would burst out laughing any second.

"Sounds like you're more a savage than a sadist," I said.

"You're right there."

I didn't expect him to know the English word, so I was a little taken by surprise.

"I didn't think you'd know that word," I said.

"I have quite a vocabulary of grim words," he said, and smiled his shy, crooked smile. Completely mad, I thought, but I couldn't suppress my desire to let him do with me whatever he wanted. I put my arms on the counter, cocked my chin up, and let Shiba-san stroke my neck.

"Hey, Shiba-san. Stop hitting on my girl." Ama's goofy voice cut in between us.

13

"I'm just checking out her skin. For when I do the tattoo."

"Oh." Ama's face visibly relaxed. After that, Ama and I bought a few earrings, and Shiba-san saw us out the door.

         •

I had gotten used to walking the streets alongside Ama. He wore three 4g pointed earrings in his left eyebrow and another three in his bottom lip. And as if that didn't make him stand out enough, he wore a tank top that made his dragon tattoo visible and his red hair was cropped so short on the sides that it looked like a thick Mohawk. When I first saw Ama at that dark techno club, I thought he looked scary. It was my first time in a club that played music other than hip-hop or trance, as most other clubs I'd been to with friends had been events. Until then I'd pretty much thought all clubs were the same. That night, after I had parted from a friend, a black guy speaking heavily accented English talked me into going. It was a club all right, but totally different from the kind I was used to. I'd become tired of the unfamiliar songs and was sitting at the bar drinking when I saw Ama dancing in a weird kind of way. He stood out, even in such a strange crowd. Our eyes met and he walked straight up to me and I remember being surprised that even people like him try to pick up girls. We made small talk for a while, but then he got me interested with his forked tongue. I remember being mesmerized by his slim, serpentine tongue, and even now I don't really understand why it attracted me so much.

I touched the tongue stud with my finger. Every now and then it came into contact with my teeth, letting out a tiny click. The pain was still there, but the swelling had gone down quite a bit. Ama turned around and looked me in the eye.

"So, Lui, how does it feel to be one step closer to having a forked tongue?"

"I'm not really sure. But I think I'm happy about it."

"Good. I want to share this feeling with you," he said with a sloppy smile.

I couldn't pinpoint exactly what was so sloppy about his smile. Perhaps it was something to do with the way his lip sagged with the weight of the piercings. Until then, my image of guys like Ama was that they spent all

15

their time being stoned and sleeping around, but I guess not all of them are like that. Ama was always kind and occasionally said sentimental things that didn't match his appearance at all. Once we got back to his room he kissed me for what felt like an eternity. He ran his forked tongue along my tongue stud, and the pain that vibrated through my body felt good. As we were having sex, I closed my eyes and thought of Shiba-san and what he had said. *A right reserved for gods alone, huh. Fine then, I guess I just have to become a god.* The sound of heavy breathing resonated in the cold space. It was summer, the air conditioner wasn't on and my body was damp with sweat, but for some reason the room was still cold. Perhaps it was because Ama only had steel furniture.

"Can I come?" Ama's wheezing voice floated lazily in the air. I opened my eyes slightly and gave a light nod. Then he pulled out and came on my crotch.

"I told you to come on my stomach."

"Sorry, I mistimed it," he said apologetically, and pulled over the box of tissues. It really pisses me off that he does that, because it makes my pubic hair all hard and matted. I just want to let the post-coital sleep kick in and let me drift off, but because of his incompetence I always end up having to take a shower.

"Use a rubber if you can't come on my stomach."

Ama looked down and apologized again. I wiped myself with a tissue and stood up.

"You taking a shower?"

Ama sounded so lonely that I stopped in my tracks.

"Uh-huh."

"Can I join you?"

I almost told him that he could. But looking at him there butt naked and wearing such a pathetic expression, I decided against it.

"No way. I'm not getting into that tiny bath with you."

I grabbed a towel, walked into the bathroom, and locked the door. I stuck my tongue out at the bathroom mirror and looked at the silver ball sitting on its tip—my first step to having a forked tongue. I thought of how Shiba-san had told me not to stretch the hole for at least a month, so there was still a long way to go.

When I came out of the bath, Ama handed me a cup of coffee.

"Thanks."

Ama smiled and watched me drink my coffee.

"Lui, let's get under the covers."

I got into the futon next to Ama. He buried his face between my breasts and began sucking my nipple. He loved to do this and it had become a kind of pre- and post-coital ritual. It always felt good when he sucked my nipples, maybe because of his forked tongue. His relaxed face made him look a little like a baby and this aroused a hint of a maternal instinct, even in the mind of someone like me. I stroked his body and he looked up at me and smiled. He looked so happy and content that watching him made me feel a little content myself. Ama had the shell of a punk, but from somewhere inside he exuded the air of an *iyashikei* TV celebrity—someone with the talent to put others at ease. He really was a difficult one to figure out.

                ·

"Wow! Unbelievable! I can't believe you did that! It must have hurt like hell."

That was my friend Maki's reaction to my pierced tongue. She kept staring at it and pulling a face, saying "ouch" over and over again.

"I mean, what came over you? You? With a tongue stud? I thought you hated all those punks and über-funky Harajuku kids."

Maki's the epitome of a Barbie-girl and a good friend of mine. We met two years ago at a club and we've been great friends ever since. We always hang out together, so she knows my tastes well.

"Well, I met this guy who's kind of a punk," I explained, "and I guess I was kind of influenced by him."

"It's unusual for a Barbie-girl like you to have a tongue stud though," she said, "I mean, first you go and stretch the holes in your ears and now you put a hole through your tongue. Do you think you're going to go totally punk?"

"Maki—I'm *not* a Barbie-girl," I retorted, but she wasn't listening to me. She just kept going on about punk this and punk that. I guess I can understand her reaction a little. I mean, if you think about it I guess a tongue stud isn't exactly the usual complement to a camisole dress and blond curls. But so what if it isn't? Anyway, it's not going to be a tongue stud forever. It's going to be the tongue of a snake.

"Maki, what do you think about tattoos?"

"Tattoos? I think tattoos can be cute. Like a little butterfly or rose or something like that, you know," she said with a smile.

19

"I don't mean the cutesy stuff. I'm thinking about dragons, tribal patterns, ukiyoe woodblock prints, that kind of thing."

"Huh?" she said, raising her voice and furrowing her brow. "What's going on with you? Is that new punk of yours trying to make you get one? Are you two an item or something? Has he completely brainwashed you?"

Actually, I couldn't help but wonder if it was brainwashing of a kind. The moment I'd laid eyes on Ama's tongue, I'd felt a shudder inside as all my morals and values started crashing to the ground. I couldn't take my eyes off it. And although the fascination didn't translate directly into a desire to possess a forked tongue myself, I had embarked on the tongue-splitting journey anyway, in hopes of finding out what it was that gave me such a rush.

"So, you want to meet him?"

Two hours later we were standing at our meeting place.

"There he is."

Maki's eyes opened wide when she saw who I was waving to.

"You've got to be kidding," she muttered.

"That's him," I said. "The red-haired monkey."

"Tell me it's not. He looks kind of scary."

As Ama came closer he could see Maki was feeling uncomfortable, so he gave her a timid look and said, "Sorry I'm so scary-looking." To my relief, that was just enough to break the ice, and Maki cracked up laughing. After that the three of us wandered downtown and ended up at some place with nothing much going for it other than that it was cheap.

"Have you noticed how everyone gets out of the way when we're walking with Ama-san?" said Maki.

"I know. When I'm walking with Ama, the scouts for the hostess bars stay out of my face and nobody tries to stuff flyers in my hand."

"So I guess I'm pretty handy to have around, huh?"

Ama and Maki immediately hit it off, and when he showed her his forked tongue, she did a complete turn-around and went off about how cool it was.

"So Lui's going to get one of these as well, huh?"

"Right. We're going to get matching tongues. Hey,

21

Lui, why don't you get your eyebrows and lips pierced as well. Then we'd have matching everything."

"No way. All I want is a forked tongue and a tattoo."

"Come on, don't turn her into a complete punk," said Maki. "Lui and me made an oath to remain Barbie-girls forever."

"Did not. Besides, I've never been a Barbie-girl."

"Yeah, right," said Ama and Maki pretty much at the same time. "You're the ultimate Barbie-girl."

Then for some reason they both looked at me and began chanting, "Down in one! Down in one!"

•

The three of us stepped out into the night air pissed out of our minds, not giving a shit about the noise we made as we shouted and cackled our way to the station through streets refreshingly empty of scumbag scouts. Almost empty, that is.

A couple of thugs came into sight, and they began to eyeball Ama as we got closer. It came as no surprise to me. Guys like them were always trying to pick a fight with him for any reason they could pull out of the air. "What you looking at?" they'd spit. Or walk into him on purpose, turn around, and bark, "Watch where you're fucking going." But all Ama ever did was laugh like a fool and apologize. The only thing tough about him was his looks—or so I thought.

One of the guys—decked out from head to toe in Versace—walked right up to me and said, "Hey, girl! That your boyfriend?" Ama and Maki were no use at all, with Maki hiding behind us and avoiding eye contact and Ama just glaring, so I just tried to walk around the guy. But he stepped over to block my path, and said, "He's not, right?"

"What? Haven't you got enough imagination to picture us fucking?" I shrugged, stone-faced. He put his arm around my shoulder and said, "No, you're right. I can't picture it." Then he pushed his hand down past my shoulder and slid it over my breast. As I was trying to remember what color bra I had on, I heard something like a dull thud and suddenly he was gone. I looked around me, not knowing what had happened. Then my eyes found him on the ground and Ama standing next to him, his eyes burning. I knew then that Ama had hit him.

23

"What the fuck are you doing?" shouted the other guy mid-stride as he came straight for Ama. Ama responded by crushing his fist into the oncoming face and then moved straight to straddle the Versace guy who was still flat out on the ground. Ama punched him in the temple, then again, then again, then again. And when the blood started to flow, Ama still didn't stop. The guy was out cold, but Ama kept on, relentless. Maki saw the blood and started to scream. That was the exact same moment I remembered that Ama was wearing thick rings on the middle and forefinger of his right hand. The sickening rhythm of metal on bone sent a chill through my body.

"Ama, come on. That's enough." I said. But he didn't seem to hear me at all, and his fist kept lunging back again and again into Versace's sticky, unflinching face.

The other guy got up and began to steal away. I knew that he would be calling the police.

"I said, that's enough!" I grabbed Ama's left shoulder, then felt the jolt of his arm as his fist went into the guy's face yet again. I looked away to the side, and all I could see was Maki throwing up. "Ama!" I shouted. Then I felt his muscles relax and I breathed a breath of relief as I thought it was all over. But it wasn't, not quite. Ama put

24

his fingers in the guy's mouth! Rummaging around in there like he was looking for something. "What the fuck are you doing!" I slapped him on the top of his head and pulled as hard as I could on his tank top. Then I heard the sound of sirens.

I looked over at Maki and shouted at her to get out of there quick. She looked as white as a ghost, but still managed to say, "Well, the three of us should get together soon, yeah." She gave a quick wave and was gone. Tough girl, Maki. She even runs well when she's drunk. I turned back to Ama, who was staggering to his feet and staring at me with a hollow gaze.

"You've gotta get a grip! Do you understand? The police are coming. We've got to go!" I tapped him on the shoulder and he gave me a gushing smile. He grabbed my hand and we ran, with him pulling away ahead, dragging me gasping for breath behind him.

After a while, when I thought I couldn't go any farther, we found a narrow alley, ducked down it, and collapsed to the ground.

"What the fuck was that!" I surprised myself with the strain in my voice.

Ama squatted down beside me, stuck out his bloody fist, and opened it in front of me to show two red

25

centimeter-long objects sitting in his palm. I instantly knew they were the guy's teeth. I felt as if an ice cube had been dropped down my back.

"They're for you. Little tokens of revenge," said Ama with a smile that was proud yet innocent, like that of a child.

"What the hell would I want with those!" I shouted, but he grabbed my arm and dropped them both into my palm, keeping his eyes on mine, saying, "Take them. They're a symbol of my love for you."

I couldn't believe what I was hearing. I didn't know what to say. I just opened my mouth and let the words come out, "That's no symbol of love. At least not in Japan."

Then he cuddled up to me and I ruffled his hair until we had both calmed down.

After that, we sauntered over to the park and found a tap where Ama washed his tank top and hands. Then we caught the last train back to Ama's place. As soon as we walked into his apartment, I pushed him into the bathroom. Then once I was alone, I took the teeth from my makeup bag and rolled them around in my palm. I washed the blood off them in the kitchen sink and stuffed them back in my bag.

I wondered how I got there. Into a situation like this with a psycho who thinks we're together. And what if I tried to leave him? Would he try to kill me?

When Ama came out of the bath, he sat next to me and looked at me like he was trying to read my thoughts. I just sat there saying nothing and eventually I heard him say, "Sorry," in a voice barely above a whisper. "It's just that I can't control myself," he said. "I mean, I'm basically good-natured, but once I cross a line it's like I have to go on to the end. Until he's dead, you know."

His words made me think that he'd killed someone before.

"Ama, you're an adult, you know. I mean in terms of the law. If you kill someone, you *will* go to prison."

"No, actually, I'm still a minor," he replied, looking me straight in the eyes. I felt myself starting to run out of patience and wondering why I even bothered worrying about him.

"Don't be so stupid."

"No, it's true!" he said.

27

"You told me you were twenty-four when we first met!"

"Yeah, but only because I thought that was how old you are. Didn't want you to think I was a kid. I kind of dropped that on you out of the blue, didn't I? Should I have broken it to you more seriously? How old are you, anyway?"

"How rude can you get? I'm still a minor too."

"You're kidding," said Ama, opening his eyes wide. "You serious? Well, that's perfect." He smiled from ear to ear and gave me a hug.

"It just means we both look old for our age," I said, pushing him away and realizing just how very little we really knew about each other. We didn't know about each other's upbringing or each other's age. It wasn't even like we'd been avoiding these topics or anything, either. They just never came up. Even now, as we found out we were both under twenty, we still didn't bother to find out exactly how old we were.

"So, Ama, what's your real name? Amano? Suama?"

"Suama? What kind of name's that? It's Amadeus. Ama's my first name and Deus is my last name. Isn't Deus a cool name? Sounds like Zeus, doesn't it?"

"If you don't want to tell me your name, that's fine with me."

"It *is* my real name. What's yours?"

"I bet you think its Lui for Louis the Fourteenth, don't you? Well, you're wrong. It's Lui for Louis Vuitton."

"So you're quite a high society woman then," he said sarcastically, while handing me the first of several beers, over which we chatted until early morning.

●

The next day, just after noon, I was over at Desire with Shiba-san, looking at tattoo designs. I couldn't believe how many there were, from ukiyoe for a certain unwelcome section of society, to skulls, to Western designs like the original Mickey Mouse. I was really impressed with the range of his drawing skills.

"You want a dragon?" asked Shiba-san, peering over my shoulder, as I thumbed through dozens of pages of dragon designs.

"Yeah, I think I might go with a dragon. This is the one Ama's got, right?"

29

"Yeah. The shape's a little different, but it's based on the same design."

Shiba-san leaned against the counter and looked down at me, while I carried on flipping through the files.

"Ama doesn't know you're here, does he?"

I looked up. Shiba-san had a thin smile on his face and a lecherous gleam in his eyes.

"No, he doesn't," I said.

"Don't tell him I told you my cell number," said Shiba-san, his expression turning a little more serious. I guessed he knew something of Ama's temper.

"What is Ama . . . ?" I started, but stopped myself.

"You want to know about him?" he asked with a shrug. Shiba-san smiled up at the ceiling for a second before bringing his gaze back down to meet mine.

"No, actually, perhaps I don't," I said.

"Fine," he said with indifference. He then came out from behind the counter and walked out of the store. Then ten seconds later the door opened and he walked back in.

"What were you doing?"

"I closed the store. I have an important customer."

"Oh, okay," I said indifferently, and looked back down at the file. Later, we went to the back room to discuss the kind of tattoo I wanted while Shiba-san drew beautiful designs with amazing speed. As someone with no artistic talent whatsoever, I was envious of his skill.

"To be honest, though, I'm still wavering. I mean, tattoos are for life, so if I'm going to get one, I want to get the best possible design there is, you know."

I leaned my chin against my fist and traced with my finger the dragon Shiba-san had drawn for me.

"True. I mean, these days there's laser removal, but basically, there's no going back. Although in my case, all I have to do is grow my hair out," he said, tracing his finger along the flying dragon on his head.

"That's not the only place you have a tattoo, though, right?"

"No. You wanna see the rest?" He grinned at me.

I gave a small nod and he pulled off his long-sleeved T-shirt to reveal a body like a canvas, with every inch covered in colors and lines, then turned around to show me his back with a dragon, a boar, a deer, butterflies, peonies, cherry blossoms, and a pine tree.

"An *Inoshikacho*[1]!" I said.

"Yeah, I like *hanafuda* cards."

---

[1] A prized combination of cards in the game of *hanafuda*, comprising a wild boar, deer, and butterfly.

"But you're missing the bush clover and red maple leaves."

"I know. Unfortunately I ran out of space."

I was surprised by his nonchalance about the whole thing, and then he turned back to me and I caught sight of another animal on his upper arm, with a single horn on its head.

"Is that a Kirin?" I asked

"Yeah. It's my favorite," he said. "It's a sacred animal. It doesn't step on fresh forage or eat raw food. I guess that you could say that it's a god of the animal kingdom."

"I don't remember the Kirin having one horn, though."

"Well, the Kirin is a legend that comes from China, and they say it has a single horn enclosed in flesh."

"That's what *I* want," I said, staring at the Kirin on his upper arm.

Shiba-san was uncharacteristically at a loss for words for a moment; then he told me, "The guy who did this was one of Japan's master tattoo artists." He paused. "I've never done a Kirin myself."

"Well, can I get him to do it for me?"

"You could," he replied. "If he wasn't dead," he added, with no trace of humor, staring into my eyes. "He burned himself to death, holding a picture of a Kirin in his arms. That's just *so* Akutagawa Ryunosuke. Some people say he shouldn't have been tattooing a sacred animal like that in the first place; that maybe he incited its rage. Who knows, maybe if you get a Kirin, Lui, you'll be damned too." Shiba-san stroked his Kirin tattoo as he said this. Neither of us said anything for a moment, and I let my eyes linger on the Kirin.

"Anyway," he continued, "a Kirin is a combination of a deer, a bull, a wolf, and a whole load of other animals. It's a real pain in the ass to draw."

"But it's what I want. Please, Shiba-san. I mean, if nothing else, at least you could draw a template for me," I pleaded.

Looking a little pissed off, Shiba-san clicked his tongue and muttered, "Oh, all right then, I'll do it,"

"Yes! Thank you, Shiba-san."

"I'll draw the template for the time being. What do you want in the background?"

I thought about it awhile, then flipped through the files again.

"This one," I said, tapping a design with my nail. "And I want to combine it with Ama's dragon."

Shiba-san gazed at the dragon for a moment, then

33

said, "I see," to himself more than to me. "It's the first time I'm doing a Kirin, so I guess it would be easier for me to combine it with something else after all."

"I want it to be about the same size as Ama's and I want it to be just on my back. How much would it cost?"

He pretended to think about it, giving a theatrical pause, then said, "Hmm . . . how about . . . one fuck," looking at me from the corner of his eye.

"That's all?" I shot him a sideward glance, and saw him glaring at me, the sadist in him coming to the surface.

"Take off your clothes," he ordered.

So I stood up, my sleeveless dress sticking to my body with sweat. I lowered the zipper and felt a breeze of cold air on my back. Then I let it slip to the ground. He looked me up and down with what looked like total disinterest, then said, "You're really thin. You know if you put on weight after a tattoo, the skin stretches and makes it look awful."

I took off my bra and panties, which were both damp with sweat. Then I slipped off my mules and sat down on the bed.

"That won't be a problem," I said. "My weight hasn't changed in years."

Shiba-san stubbed out his cigarette in the ashtray and stepped up toward the bed, undoing his belt as he walked. He stopped at the edge of the bed and pushed me down roughly with one hand, then brought his palm up against my neck. His fingers traced my veins and his grip tightened until his thin fingertips began to dig into my flesh. All the while, he was still standing, staring down at me. The veins on his right arm bulged to the surface. My body was screaming out for air, and I began twitching. My face tightened and my throat felt like it would crack.

He said, "I like that. Seeing you suffer makes me so hard."

Shiba-san let go of my throat and pulled off his pants and boxers. I was still feeling woozy and light-headed when he got up onto the bed, pressed his knees down on my shoulders, and stuck his cock toward my mouth— framing my face with a dancing dragon on either thigh. I took his sour cock into my mouth and noticed the smell of his body. I've always liked sex in the summer more than any other season. I think it's that sour, sweet smell of sweat and ammonia. Shiba-san looked down at me with a blank expression, grabbed hold of my hair, and pulled on it in a rough rhythm—fucking my face. I could feel myself getting wet, though he hadn't even laid a finger on me. How very convenient, I thought.

"So how does Ama do you?" he asked, pulling his hips upward.

"How does anyone do anyone?"

Shiba-san shrugged. Then his eyes moved to his pants, from which he pulled off the belt to use to tie my hands behind me. "Don't you get frustrated?"

"Not really. I can come having sex the regular way."

"Are you saying you think I can't?"

"Well, can you?"

"No."

"That's because you're a pyscho sadist."

"I can get off on guys too, though, you know. I've got quite a range," he laughed.

Him saying that made me think of him and Ama fucking, and I thought that might actually be quite beautiful. Shiba-san picked me up in his thin arms and put me down on the floor. Then he sat down on the bed and stuck his right foot in my face. I sucked his toes one by one starting with the big toe, and then licked his foot until my mouth was completely dry. My neck started to hurt because I had been crouching without leaning my hand against anything. Shiba-san grabbed my hair again and pulled my face up. I suspected I was gazing up at him with empty eyes. Veins were popping out on the surface of his cock.

"You wet?"

I nodded slightly, and Shiba-san picked me up and sat me on the bed. Almost instinctively, I spread my legs and felt a slight tension sweep through my body. I've been with sadists before, and you never know what they're going to do. I've had enemas, which were fine, and I've played around with toys. I've also got no qualms with spanking or anal. What I don't want to see, however, is blood. I remember once I let a guy put a small glass bottle in me, which he then tried to smash with a hammer. And there'd even been some real weirdos that got a kick out of poking me with needles.

I could feel that my wrists and palms were damp, and I was getting goose bumps on my shoulders and upper arms, but I felt a genuine sense of relief as it slowly became obvious that Shiba-san had no intention of incorporating anything else. He stuck two fingers up inside me and pistoned them in and out a few times before extracting them and wiping them against my thigh, like he'd touched something dirty. I stole a look at his expression, and when I did, I felt myself getting even wetter still.

"Put it in me," I pleaded.

He took his two still-wet fingers he'd wiped against my thigh, stuck them in my mouth, and moved them around.

"Taste gross?"

I nodded and he pulled them out, plugged them back in my pussy, then returned them to my mouth. It brought back an immediate mental picture of Ama rummaging through that guy's mouth in Shinjuku.

"That unbearable?"

I nodded again and he pulled out his fingers, placed a hand on my head, and pushed it down into the sheets, causing my body to tremble as I tried to support my weight with my head, shoulders, and knees.

"Please, just put it in," I begged.

"Shut up!" he said sharply, then grabbed my hair, grinding my head down against the pillow. His arm reached around me roughly and he pulled my hips up high. Then he spat on my vagina, rammed his fingers in again, moved them around roughly, then slammed his cock into me. Right from the beginning, he pounded me deep and hard, my whispered gasps echoing through the musty, clammy air, and in no time I found myself crying real tears—something I do easily when it feels really good. Gradually I was getting there, I could sense the feeling in me building. As he continued to pound and slap against me, he loosened the grip of the belt around my wrists. Then, when my hands were free, he quickly pulled out his cock and I felt the trickle of a tear run from the corner of my eye. Then he grabbed me roughly again, pulled me on top, grabbed an ass cheek in each hand with a clawlike grip, and dragged my whole body back and forth. By now, my entire vagina was numb.

"I want to see more tears," he barked at me, instantly causing more tears to well up in my eyes.

"I'm coming," I murmured, rocking my hips back and forth violently with new urgency.

After I'd come, I could hardly move. But Shiba-san simply pushed me over, climbed on top, then slammed himself into me in a hard, unforgiving rhythm—grabbing my hair, choking me, and smiling all the while from the cruel pleasure it gave him. Then he said, "Here it comes," just the way he had when he pierced my tongue, shoving his cock in deep, pulling out, then climbing up my body to

39

dump his cum in my mouth. I felt a strange combination of relief and excitement, like I'd been released from Hell, but exiled from Heaven at the same time.

Shiba-san got off the bed, wiped his cock with a tissue, and put on his boxers. He threw the box of tissues in my direction, which I caught, and as I wiped off the cum, I looked at myself in the mirror, tinged with running makeup and tears. After I'd finished up, we sat on the bed, leaned up against the wall, and stared at the ceiling while smoking cigarettes. We sat there doing nothing for a while, only uttering minimal exchanges like "Can you pass the ashtray," or "It's hot, huh?"

After a while, Shiba-san stood up, turned around and looked at me with disdain. "If you break up with Ama, you become my girl, all right?"

I almost burst out laughing. "You'd probably kill me!"

"And Ama won't?" said Shiba-san, chillingly without a change in expression.

For a moment I was lost for words.

"But if we did get together," he continued, "it would be with marriage in mind." He threw my bra and panties to me and I slipped my panties on. I tried to imagine what married life with Shiba-san would be like, and whether it would be something I'd be likely to survive. Then I slipped my dress back on and got off the bed. Shiba-san took a small can of coffee from a mini fridge, opened it, and handed it to me.

"Underneath it all, you're a nice guy, aren't you?"

"I only opened it because your nails are so damn long."

I pecked him on the cheek and said, "Thank you." Words of gratitude that seemed totally at odds with where we sat. I imagined my "thank you" floating around forever with nowhere to go. Then Shiba-san went back to the store and reopened it for business.

"Do you ever actually get any customers?" I asked.

"Yeah. It's just most people come for body piercing or tattoos, so they make reservations. It's not the sort of shop where people tend to stop by and browse."

"I see."

I sat down on a seat behind the counter and stuck out my tongue. I touched the stud with my finger. It didn't hurt anymore.

"Hey, you think I can put in a 12 now?"

"Not yet. You have to keep it in for about a month. That's why I told you to use a 12 for your starter stud," said Shiba-san coldly, peeping behind the counter from out on the store floor.

"Will you call me when you finish the design?"

"Sure. Come with Ama. Tell him you want to go look at earrings. Then I'll show you the design and you can act all surprised, like you've never seen it or thought of it before."

"Call me during the day—when Ama's at work."

"Yeah, yeah, I know," he said, and went back to organizing stuff on a rack.

I put my hand on my bag to go home, and then Shiba-san suddenly turned around to face me.

I stopped abruptly. "What?"

"I think I might be a child of God," he said without changing his expression.

"Child of God? Isn't that the title of some crappy B-movie?"

"No. Think about it. God has to be a sadist to give people life."

"So I guess you're saying Mary was a masochist?"

"Yeah. Guess so," murmured Shiba-san, and he turned to face the rack again. I picked up my bag and walked out from behind the counter.

"You wanna grab a bite before you go?"

"No, Ama will be getting home soon."

"Fine. I'll see you then." He patted my head roughly. I took his right arm and stroked the Kirin.

"I'll do you a really cool design," he said.

I smiled, gave a small wave, and headed out. Outside, the sun was setting and the air was so fresh I almost choked. I took the train back to Ama's place. The shopping promenade on the way home from the station was full of too many families. In fact the sound of all those voices made me want to vomit. A small child bumped into me and the mother pretended not to notice. I kept my eye on the kid, though, until he looked up and saw me. When our eyes met, I swear he was just about to cry, so I just tutted at him and kept on walking. I really didn't want to live in this kind of world. I wanted to live recklessly and leave nothing behind but ashes in this dark, dull world.

As soon as I got back to Ama's place I put my clothes in the washing machine and turned it on because Desire always smells of incense and the scent gets into my clothes whenever I've been there. I stepped into the shower and washed myself thoroughly from head to toe. When I got

43

out, I dried myself down and put on a pair of jeans and one of Ama's T-shirts. After putting on a little makeup and drying my hair, I went and hung my dress out to dry, then sat down to take a break just as the doorknob turned and Ama walked in.

"Hi."

"Hi."

I was relieved to see him smiling broadly.

"I was sleepy all day long," said Ama, stretching.

It wasn't surprising he was tired considering we'd been drinking until the early morning. I was exhausted too, as I couldn't get back to sleep after seeing Ama out in the morning—that's when I decided to call Shiba-san. My entire day had gone like clockwork—as predictable as the passage of time itself. The only thing special about my day was the encounter with the Kirin. Now I just couldn't wait until it decorated my skin.

I didn't care if Ama was Amadeus. Shiba-san was a son of God, and I was the only unexceptional one among us. All I wanted was to be part of an underground world where the sun doesn't shine, there are no serenades, and the sound of children's laughter is never, ever heard.

Ama and I ate dinner at a pub, went back to the room, and had sex. Almost straight after, Ama fell into a deep sleep, as if he had been knocked out. I cracked open a beer and sipped it while looking at his sleeping face, wondering to myself whether he'd kill me the way he had that sleazy guy if he knew me and Shiba-san had been fucking. Then I thought that if I really had to choose, I guess I'd rather be killed by a son of God than by Amadeus, although I didn't really think that this particular son of God could ever kill anyone.

I turned my attention to Ama's arm and the way it hung down from the bed, the silver rings on his fingers catching the light. I tried to erase the thought from my mind by turning on the TV. I flipped through brain-dead variety shows and comatose documentaries for a while before turning the TV off. The only magazines Ama had at his place were men's fashion magazines, and I didn't know how to use his computer, or any other for that matter. I looked around the room clucking my tongue, looking for something to do, and picked up a newspaper. It was a trashy sports tabloid that was actually pretty much my primary source of information. I checked the late-night TV listings on the back page, and then flicked through page by page, working my way back to the front.

All I really got out of it was that people were being murdered every day here in Japan, and that even the sex trade was feeling the pinch of the recession. As I was flipping through the pages, a headline jumped out at me: 29-YEAR-OLD GANGSTER BEATEN TO DEATH IN SHINJUKU.

The face of the guy from the night before came straight to mind. Though surely he was older than twenty-nine, with that face. If not, he looked much too old for his age, kind of like Ama and I. It must have been a similar incident somewhere else. After all, Shinjuku is a pretty big place. I took a deep breath and continued to read the article.

The victim died upon arrival at the hospital. Police say the murderer is yet to be found. According to a witness, the man has red hair, a slight build and is about 175 to 180cm tall.

I looked at Ama, compared him with the description in the article, and put down the paper. If the suspect in the article really was Ama, then wouldn't the witness have mentioned the tattoo and the face full of piercings? Of course they would, I told myself. It must just be some guy who happens to look a little similar to Ama, that's all. The guy Ama beat up would still be alive, I was sure of it. Anyway, I grabbed my handbag, left the room, and walked quickly to the convenience store, where I bought bleach and ash-colored hair dye. When I got back, Ama was still sound asleep, so I shook him awake.

"Huh? What's up? What're you doing?" he mumbled.

I slapped his head and made him sit down in front of the mirror.

"What? What are you gonna do?"

"What do you mean 'What are you gonna do?' We're going to change your hair. That disgusting red hair of yours has really got to go."

Ama took off all his clothes except his boxers, just as I told him.

"Red hair doesn't go with dark skin, didn't anyone ever tell you that? You've got no taste, have you?"

And as I grimaced at the fumes from the bleach I was mixing, Ama smiled and said, "You're so kind. I'll do my best to improve my sense of style. With your help of course."

I was relieved that Ama had interpreted my actions positively and I thought he must be an optimist at heart.

"Yeah, whatever," I said, and began brushing the

bleach onto his hair, which I'd divided into sections with a comb. I used half the container of it. Of course, changing his hair color wasn't really going to change anything, but for now I thought we should at least change what we could.

Once Ama's hair was rinsed and blow-dried, it had gone from red to blond. I remembered once being told by a hairdresser that when you go from one hair color to a completely different one, like from red to ash, you needed to be really thorough in taking the first color out. So I mixed the rest of the bleach and repeated the entire process, turning Ama's hair to a whitish blond. I blow-dried it again until it was stiff, and then I applied the ash-colored dye. Ama must have been really sleepy because he kept nodding off all the way through. I must admit I did feel a little sorry for him, but after all it *was* for his own good. Once I'd finished applying the dye and wrapping cling film around his head, he smiled at me with a vacant kind of stare.

"Thank you, Lui," he said.

For a second I wondered whether I should show him

the article, but then I decided against it and headed to the bathroom to wash my hands.

"Do you think I could pass as a half-decent-looking guy now?"

"I never said you looked bad," I said, poking my head out of the bathroom.

Ama laughed, "You know I'd shave my head for you if you wanted. I'd even dress like a Barbie-boy to match you. Even if you told me to lose the tan and whiten my skin, then you know I would."

"Get real, Ama."

He wasn't bad-looking. I mean, all right, his eyes do have a kind of constant glare that can be uncomfortable, but in general I'd still say he falls into the good-looking category. Still, with the tattoo and a face full of piercings, I guess it was kind of difficult to really tell if he looked good or bad. In fact, if I didn't know him at all and I just saw him in the street, I'd probably think, *What a waste of a pretty face*. I do know how he feels, though. After all, I wanted people to judge me by my appearance too. I often like to think that if sunlight reached into everywhere on the entire planet, I'd find a way to turn myself into a shadow.

About ten minutes after I applied the dye, Ama started to fidget and kept asking, "Is it done yet?" I guess I could have been a bit more sympathetic to him, but I was determined to get every last trace of red out of his hair, so in the end I left the dye in for more than thirty minutes. Then, after taking the wrap off his head, I scruffled his hair with my hand.

"What are you doing?" he asked.

"I'm oxidizing it. Exposing it to the air makes the color set deeper."

After making sure that the color was nice and even, I said, "All set," and handed him a bath towel.

"All right," said Ama, and he sloped off to the bathroom. Then while I waited for him to finish his shower I took another look at the newspaper. I kept telling myself that it couldn't be Ama, so I couldn't really understand why I was letting it get me all worked up, especially since I didn't even like him that much.

When Ama came out of the shower, I styled his hair. He looked at me in the mirror, batted his eyelids, and smiled.

"Stop that." I said, "It makes me cringe," and he frowned and turned toward me.

Ama's hair was now the color of ash. There wasn't a trace of red left in it. "Ama, starting tomorrow, you are always going to wear long-sleeved shirts."

"Why? It's still hot."

"Shut up. People always mistake you for a gangster because of your tank tops."

"Okay then," said Ama, looking a little hurt.

I had to get him to hide those tattoos away. They stuck out like a sore thumb, and the police might not be mentioning anything about them for some special reason. Though maybe I was just overreacting or reading too much into things.

Either way, I managed to get him to listen, and though he looked totally bewildered by all my sudden demands, he hung his head and said, "Okay, I promise," then held me tight in his arms and whispered, "Anything for you, Lui."

And as he dragged me into bed, I thought to myself again how he just didn't look like a murderer. He just didn't look like one. So I told myself that everything was all right and that Ama was just a goofy idiot who would always be laughing by my side. Once we were in bed, he pulled up my dress and sucked one of my nipples. After a little while, I felt the sucking grow weaker and his breathing growing deep. I pulled down my dress, turned off the light, and closed my eyes. In the dark, I found myself praying, though to who I'm not really sure. In no time at all, sleep had enveloped me.

The next day at around noon I was woken by the sound of my phone. It was the manager of a companion company I'd done some work for in the past, and though I was enjoying having a bit of a break from that kind of work, the manager said another girl had canceled late so I found myself reluctantly accepting a job for the evening. Actually, I think my reluctance must have showed in my voice, because the manager went up from my normal rate and offered me ¥30,000 for it, which was pretty good.

Until then I'd been living off Ama's money for quite a while, even considering packing in work altogether and just depending on him. But I got to my feet to get ready. After all, ¥30,000 could get us both nicely drunk out of our minds.

I first got into the companion thing about six months ago because it was just so easy. All you had to do was register with an agency, and you always got paid on the day. You got ¥10,000 for pouring drinks and basically looking pretty at hotel parties for a couple of hours. I felt fortunate to have been born with a face people liked.

I met up with the manager and the other girls in the hotel lobby. I was a bit late, so I think the manager was getting a little concerned, but his face visibly relaxed when he saw me, breaking into a smile and saying, "I'm so glad you could make it." In the changing room, all of us girls were given kimonos to wear. First I helped the girls who didn't know how to put theirs on properly. When I first started, I didn't know how to put mine on either, but I taught myself by watching the others and now it came to me easily. The kimono I'd been given was bright red, and I also had to put on a straight brown wig that I'd brought with me. After all, you can't work as a companion at a respectable party with blond hair, but I wasn't about to go and dye it just for the night. Just as I was tucking the last few exposed locks of hair up into the wig, the manager came up to me and said, "Miss Nakazawa." I remember it felt funny to hear, as nobody had really used my last name in quite a long time. I was starting to forget I even had one.

"Um, your earrings . . . ," the manager said apologetically.

"Oh, right," I said, and touched my earrings. I almost forgot. It's not like it matters if you're wearing regular earrings, but my 0g ones didn't really go too well with a kimono, and they certainly wouldn't go down too well at a respectable company party. So I took off all five of them and put them in my makeup bag. As I did so, I caught a glimpse of the two teeth. I wondered again about Ama and the thug and if the police might have realized that two teeth were missing from the scene.

"Miss Nakazawa?"

It was my manager again.

Getting just a little bit annoyed, I turned around and said, "Yes?"

I don't know what he was going to say, but as I turned he looked kind of surprised and said, "Is that a stud?"

I knew he was referring to my tongue, of course.

"Yes it is."

"Well, can you take it off?"

"Well, the thing is, I just put it in. So I don't really want to take it out."

"Ahh," he said, screwing up his face and thinking what to say to that, but I cut in before he got there, saying, "Don't worry, it'll be fine. It's not like I'm going to be catching flies or anything," as I moved closer toward him with a warm smile.

"Oh, all right then," he muttered, his face relaxing as I smiled at him a little more. I could twist him around my finger with a smile, and the other girls knew it too. I guess that's why most of them don't really like me.

We went into the party hall with trays in hand and served up drinks and smiles. It was the usual boring, buffet-style dinner party. After a while I went to the back room of the hall with Yuri, one of the few girls I got along with, and pretended to be sorting out empty bottles while we drank beer and talked excitedly about tongue piercing.

"I can't believe you put a hole in your tongue."

Her reaction was very similar to Maki's.

"It was all about a guy, right?" Yuri smiled, wiggling her thumb to represent him.

"I guess so. Though I fell for the tongue rather than the actual guy."

Soon enough the talk had moved on from tongues to sex, and we'd both become kind of rowdy by the time the manager came to get us. We both took one last swig of beer, had a quick squirt of breath freshener, and went back out to the party.

At the end of the evening, I counted a total of thirteen business cards from various elite execs, and after the party was over Yuri and I looked through what we'd got.

"This looks like a good one. Managing Director." Yuri was sorting out the cards in order of her preference.

"But I don't remember his face, and he's probably some over-the-hill old guy anyway."

As for me, I had absolutely no interest in elite guys in suits, and I was sure they'd feel the same about a girl with a tongue stud. I always managed to do all right at these kinds of events, though, playing the part of a pleasant, polite Japanese girl and receiving quite a handful of business cards. But it wasn't really me they were giving the cards to. They were giving them to some character I played the part of just for the occasion. Anyway, once my tongue was properly split, I'd never be doing this kind of work again, I thought while looking at it in the mirror, looking forward to when the hole would be bigger.

After going to another party at a different hotel and doing the same thing over again, we finally got off work at eight. I went with Yuri to the office to get our pay, and then we both decided to go off to the station together. While we were walking, my cell phone rang. Yuri wiggled her thumb again, referring to my boyfriend, then raised her eyebrows and laughed. When I saw Ama's name flashing on the screen, I realized I'd forgotten to leave a note or send him a mail from my phone.

"Hello? Lui? Where are you? What are you doing?" He sounded as if he was about to cry as he fired one question at me after another.

"Sorry. I was called suddenly out to do some companion work. I'm on my way home now."

"What? I didn't know you worked. What do you mean, 'companion'?"

"Wooah. Calm down. It's just a bit of part-time. Nothing underhand."

Yuri was trying hard not to laugh as she watched me

shrink back under the heavy fire of questions. Eventually he cooled off a little and I agreed to meet him in front of the station. The moment I hung up, Yuri burst out laughing.

"He's got you on a pretty tight leash, huh?"

"Yeah, he's like a kid."

"Well, I think it's cute," she said, nudging me.

If only cute was all he was . . . , I thought, and sighed. Yuri and I then split off and went our own ways home from the station. I rode the train for twenty minutes, then skipped up the steps to the exit when I got to my station. I saw Ama standing on the other side of the ticket gate and I waved. He waved back, but he had a really pitiful expression on his face.

"I got home and you were gone! No note, no nothing! I thought you'd left me! You worried me to death," he blurted out all in one exhausting breath as soon as we had sat down and ordered beers at a *yakiniku* restaurant.

"Now we can enjoy a little luxury," I said.

Ama kept asking me about my work. Then, when he finally felt convinced that there was nothing dodgy going on, his usual smile returned to his face. "I wish I could see you in a kimono," he said, squeezing a lemon onto my dish.

The beer was going down great and the beef was delicious. It really felt like the perfect dinner. It's funny really. I mean, I'm the first person to bitch about having to work, but when you do finish work, a beer really does taste so much better. It was the only saving grace of work. I was in a good mood, and complimented Ama on his new hair color and laughed at his stupid jokes. It was a time when everything felt okay. When it seemed not a single thing could go wrong.

Summer was already over, but its heat still oozed from everywhere. About three weeks had passed since Shiba-san showed me the Kirin tattoo at Desire and I'd suddenly got a call from him. "I had a real tough time drawing it," he said before explaining exactly why in excessive detail, finishing up at last with "I can't wait to show it to you."

By then I had promoted my tongue stud to a 12g. 59

The next day I told Ama that I wanted to look at some earrings and we both headed over to Desire. When we got there, Shiba-san took us to the back room and got a piece of paper out from his desk.

"Wow, that's really something," said Ama.

He wasn't the only one to act that way either; I was totally mesmerized by it. Shiba-san could tell too. He kept showing off like a kid with a new toy saying, "Cool, huh?"

"This is what I want."

I'd made up my mind the moment I saw it. Just the thought of this glorious beast on my back made my heart beat a little bit faster. A dragon that looked as if it might fly off the paper at any moment, and a Kirin with its front legs raised high, as if ready to leap over the dragon. A pair of exquisite companions inseparable from each other, and from my life.

"Okay," said Shiba-san with a smile.

"That's great, Lui," cried Ama, taking my hands in his. I couldn't believe that the most beautiful tattoo design I'd ever seen would soon belong to me. Immediately we moved on to deciding on the size and exactly where it would go, settling on a scale of fifteen centimeters by thirty—a little smaller than Ama's—and a location extending across my back from my left shoulder toward my spine. We also decided when to begin—in just three days' time.

"Don't drink any alcohol the night before. And get to bed as early as possible. Having a tattoo like this can take a lot out of you," said Shiba-san, with Ama nodding in experienced agreement.

"Don't worry. I'll take care of her," said Ama, putting his arm around Shiba-san's shoulders, and for a split second Shiba-san glared at me the way he did when we were fucking. I glanced back at him with a smile, and I saw him struggle to suppress a smile of his own.

Afterward Ama suggested we should all go get some food. Shiba-san closed the store a little earlier than usual and the three of us stepped outside. Strangers moved out of our way as we walked along the street.

"Everyone's staring at us because of you, Shiba-san," said Ama.

"Me? What about you? Decked out like some out-of-place gangster!"

"I look more normal as a gangster than you do as a punk!"

"Don't worry, you both look scary," I said, and they both shut up.

"A gangster, a punk, and a Barbie-girl. Together we're a real fucked-up combination," said Ama, looking back and forth between me and Shiba-san.

"As I've told you before, I'm *not* a Barbie-girl," I said. "Fuck it. I want beer. Let's go to an *izakaya.*"

We walked a little further along the bustling downtown street, with me between Ama and Shiba-san, until we found a cheap *izakaya.* On entering, we took our shoes off and were led to one of the Japanese-style seating areas, while other customers shot us glances before turning away uncomfortably. We toasted with beer, then got into a heated discussion about tattoos. Ama began by telling us about his experience, and Shiba-san followed with stories or trials and tribulations from when he first became a tattoo artist to the passion he'd put into the Kirin design. By the time we were reaching the end of our meal, both of them had their tops off and were talking about the specific method used here, the kind of gradation done there, etc. Watching them brought a smile to my face. It was the first time I'd seen Shiba-san looking like he was having fun. He'd never shown me that side of himself when we were alone, but I guess even sadists smile from ear to ear sometimes.

As for me, the beers were going down well and I was

getting a little rowdy, shouting, "Put your clothes back on!" at them and telling them to shut the fuck up. All in all, it was a fun dinner with cold beer and a beautiful design on my mind. Like those three things were all I needed.

When Ama got up to go to the bathroom, Shiba-san leaned over and stroked my head.

"No complaints, right?"

"None whatsoever," I said. We smiled and looked into each other's eyes.

"I'll tattoo it beautifully," he said, with a strength in his voice that made me feel glad to have met him.

"It shouldn't be too difficult with your skills," I said.

"The hand of God," said Shiba-san, with a wry smile, opening up the hand he had placed on the table. "But what should I do if I find myself suddenly overcome with the desire to kill you?" His eyes turned cold as he stared at his hand.

"Then that would be that, I guess," I said, before taking in a mouthful of beer. As I did so, I glimpsed Ama coming back from the bathroom.

"Good. Because I've never felt such a strong desire to

63

kill anyone," said Shiba-san, just a fraction of a second before Ama sat back down with a big, sloppy smile on his face.

"The toilet was covered in puke. I almost threw up when I saw it."

With Ama's words, the atmosphere quickly returned to normal. Well, at least as normal as it could be considering I was sitting between a guy who'd beat someone beyond recognition for me and another who wanted to kill me. I wondered if there'd ever come a day when one of them would kill me.

•

Two days later, Ama took all the alcoholic drinks out of the fridge and put them into the kitchen cabinet. Then he chained it shut with a padlock.

"What are you doing? You're acting like I'm some kind of alcoholic," I said.

"Well, you are—pretty much," said Ama as he slipped the key into his pocket. "Now, don't you go buying beer at the convenience store while I'm out," he said, as he left for work.

What did he think I was? Some kind of half-wit? Of course I could go without alcohol for a day, I thought, and gave the cabinet a small nudge with my elbow. By the time Ama got home that night, however, I must admit I could think of nothing but beer. Not surprising, though, really. I mean, I'd been drinking during the day and every night for quite a while by then. I guess it had become such a natural part of my life that I didn't really notice how much I was drinking or how addictive alcohol was. I was getting more and more irritated as time passed, and when Ama came home I took it all out on him. I guess he must have kind of expected it, though, as all he did was try to calm me down.

"I told you," he said. "You may not be aware yourself, but you're alcohol dependent."

"Oh, fuck off," I said. "It's nothing to do with a drink. It's seeing your stupid face that pisses me off!"

"Yeah, whatever you say, Lui. Just try not to think about alcohol. Have some dinner and then get to bed early. Tomorrow's the big day."

It pissed me off even more to have to be calmed down by Ama, but I got ready to go out anyway. Dinner was cheap stewed slices of beef on a bowl of rice and, of course, no beer. It was so overly sweet on its own that I had to cover it in *shichimi* to make it even vaguely appetizing. Ama annoyed me even more by looking at me like an overly protective mother the whole time. I even hit him across the head a couple of times too, but he wouldn't knock it off.

When we got home, Ama started ordering me around, telling me to do this and that. Then when I came out of the bath, he made me put on my sweats and forced me to drink a cup of warm milk he'd made with plenty of sugar. After that he dragged me into bed even though it was only eight o'clock.

"There's no way I'm going to be able to fall asleep this early. What time you think I went to bed last night?"

"Well, just try, Lui. Do you want me to count sheep for you?"

Before I could answer, he began anyway, so I just relented and closed my eyes. As he approached the one hundredth sheep, his counting trailed off, and he suddenly put his arms around me and squeezed me tight.

"Can I come with you tomorrow?"

"You have work tomorrow," I said, causing Ama to drop his head.

"Its not that I don't trust Shiba-san, but I am a bit

worried. I mean, it's going to be just the two of you, right?"

I let out a sigh. "There's nothing to worry about. He's a professional. He's not going to jump me," I said firmly.

"Okay," he said, but I could tell he wasn't happy.

"Be careful, though. I'm serious. Sometimes I just can't tell what that guy's thinking."

"Well, you know, not everyone is as easy to understand as you."

Ama laughed, but it was a weak laugh. Then he took my clothes off and made me lie on my stomach, while he kissed and caressed my back over and over again.

"So there's going to be a dragon dancing here tomorrow, huh?"

"And a Kirin."

"Seems a shame to ruin such beautiful white skin. But I'm sure you'll look even sexier with a tattoo."

He caressed my back over and over, then moved to slip into me from behind. As usual, though, he ended up coming all over my crotch, and as usual I swore at him and headed off for a shower.

When I came out, he apologized again and massaged my entire body from head to toe. My body relaxed, my consciousness blurred, and I felt sleep descend upon me. My last waking thought of the day was how I would stretch my tongue hole to a 10g before leaving home in the morning.

When I got to Desire the next day, the CLOSED sign was already up. It was hot outside and my thin dress was already damp with sweat. The door wasn't locked, and when I opened it I met eyes with Shiba-san, who was sitting behind the counter drinking coffee. "Welcome," he called out in a cheerful voice, and beckoned me to the back room, where I could see the Kirin and dragon design sitting on a table. He picked up a black leather bag, put it on the table, and slowly opened it. Inside I could see a whole collection of tools I didn't recognize. A stick with many needles on the end, for example, and all different kinds of ink.

"Sleep okay last night?"

"Yeah, Ama put me to bed at eight."

Shiba-san chuckled, and put some sheets on the bed.

"Now take your clothes off and lie down facing the cabinet," he said, taking the ink and needles out of the bag without once looking my way. So I took off my dress and bra and lay down on the bed.

"We're going to tattoo the outline today. That determines everything, so if there's anything you want to change, now's the time to tell me."

I pushed my upper body up and turned to face him.

"I have just one request. I don't want the dragon or the Kirin to have eyes."

Shiba-san looked taken aback for a second before opening his mouth.

"You mean you don't want me to draw in the pupils?"

"Yep. No eyeballs."

"But why?"

"Have you ever heard the legend of *garyoutensei*? You know, the one where the painter, Choyousou, was painting a white dragon on the walls of a temple? Anyway, when he drew in its eyes, it came to life and flew away to Heaven."

Shiba-san nodded slowly, looked up into space, and then stared back down at me.

"Okay. I understand. I won't give them eyes. But to

stop the faces from looking unbalanced, I'll probably have to use some gradation on the green around the eyes to make up for it. Would that be all right with you?"

"That'd be good. Thank you, Shiba-san."

"You're a selfish girl," he said as he sat down on the seat next to the corner of the bed and stroked my cheeks. He then shaved the fuzzy hairs from my left shoulder to my hip, disinfected my back with a piece of gauze, and traced the outline of the design onto my back using tracing paper. Then he got a mirror to show me and asked if it was okay. I told him it was fine, and he began rummaging through his tools, until he found what looked like a thick ballpoint pen with a handle on it. I assumed it was what he was going to use to do the tattoo.

I turned around and showed Shiba-san my tongue. "Look, I stretched it to a 10g," I said.

Shiba-san gave me a brilliant smile and said, "It's coming along well. Don't go too fast, though. It's not like with ears. You get your tongue infected and you'll really know what pain is."

"I'll take it steady," I said.

"It hurt, didn't it?" he said, tracing my lips with a finger.

"Yeah."

He patted my head. "Okay then. Here it comes."

He placed a cold, rubber-gloved hand on my back, and I gave a quick nod. Then almost instantly I felt a sharp pain in my back. It didn't hurt as much as I'd expected, but I couldn't stop my entire body from tensing up each time the needle broke the skin.

"Try breathing out when I put the needle in, and in when I pull it out."

I did as I was told and it became a little easier. Shiba-san kept his needles going at a steady pace all the while and finished the outline about two hours later. The whole time he was doing it, though, he didn't say a word. I glanced over at him every now and then and he was always completely focused on the job, not even bothering to wipe the sweat from his forehead. When at last he stopped the needle, he wiped down my back with a towel, then stretched and cracked his neck.

"You really take pain well, don't you? Most first-timers don't stop whining."

"Really? Maybe I'm just insensitive; frigid even."

"Yeah right. You weren't even close to frigid the other day."

He lit a cigarette, took one long drag, then placed it between my lips. Then he took out another to smoke for himself.

"Very kind of you."

"Not really," he said. "The first drag is always the best."

"I think it's the second, actually."

He chuckled just a little, but there were no words to follow.

"So did you feel the desire to kill me?"

"Yeah. I had to concentrate hard on the tattoo to keep my mind off it."

Still lying on my stomach, I stuck out my hand and flicked the ash from the tip of my cigarette into the ashtray, watching it crumple under its own weight then following other stray particles with my eyes as they floated down onto the surface of the bed.

"If you ever decide you want to die, let me kill you," said Shiba-san, putting a hand on the nape of my neck. I smiled and nodded. Then he smiled back at me and asked, "Can I fuck your dead body?"

"I don't care what happens to my body after I'm dead," I said with a shrug.

They do say dead men tell no tales after all. In that

case, surely there's nothing more meaningless than not being able to give an opinion on anything. It makes me wonder why people fork out fortunes to pay for tomb-stones. I mean, for me, I've got absolutely no interest in my body if my mind no longer lives in it. I couldn't care less if it was eaten by dogs.

"Perhaps I wouldn't be able to get it up, though—if I couldn't see you suffer."

Shiba-san grabbed my hair and pulled it upward. My neck muscles twitched with the unexpected pressure. Shiba-san grabbed my chin and made me look up.

"Want to suck it?"

I found myself nodding my head, as I didn't feel like I could, or should, say no to Shiba-san. I sat up and put my hand on his belt and he put his hands around my neck. He choked me so hard I thought he was going to kill me. The he started to fuck me—but only from behind this time, perhaps to protect my back. Even after he'd fin-ished, he kept staring at my back.

I didn't put my bra back on for obvious reasons. I just slipped on my dress; Shiba-san sat without his shirt on, watching me the entire time. I was looking around for a garbage bin to throw the cum-filled tissue into when I heard a faint noise. Shiba-san must have heard it as well, as he was frowning in the direction the noise had come from.

"Could it be a customer? Didn't you lock the door?" I asked.

"I forgot. But I put the CLOSED sign up." The moment the words left Shiba-san's mouth, the door opened.

"Lui?" said Ama, walking in.

"Hey, we just finished. Aren't you supposed to be at work?" asked Shiba-san with feigned innocence. I just stood frozen for a moment, imagining how it could have all gone wrong had he gotten here just minutes earlier.

"I got off early. Told them I had constipation."

"Your workplace lets people off early for constipation?" I asked incredulously.

"Well, the boss wasn't happy, but he still let me go," Ama replied, not catching the sarcasm in my voice. I slipped the tissue between the bedsheets, and then Ama caught a glimpse of my tattoo, getting all excited and saying, "Wow. Awesome. Thanks, Shiba-san!"

"By the way," he turned to Shiba-san, "you didn't try anything with my Lui, did you?"

"Course not. She's way too skinny for me."

Ama looked relieved.

"Hey, why is . . . ?" said Ama suddenly, not finishing his sentence, but just looking puzzled.

I looked at him, hoping he wouldn't see the guilt in my face, then stole a glance at Shiba-san who was also kind of frowning.

"Why haven't the Kirin and the dragon got eyes?"

I breathed a sigh of relief and said, "That's the way I asked for it," then went on to give him the same explanation I'd given Shiba-san earlier.

"I see," he said, "but my dragon's got eyes and it hasn't flown away."

I slapped him playfully across his head for making such a dumb remark, then pulled the strap of my dress back onto my shoulder.

"Don't take a bath for a while. Don't spray water directly onto it when you're taking a shower. Don't scrub it; dab it when you dry it with a towel. Don't forget to use the disinfectant twice a day. And after you put disinfectant on it, rub some skin cream into it too. And try not to expose it to the sun. You'll notice scabs will start to develop in about a week's time, but whatever you do, don't scratch them. Once they've fallen off and the swelling's gone down, we'll move on to the next stage. Anyway, just

75

call me when the scabs have disappeared," said Shiba-san, tapping me lightly on the shoulder.

"Will do," Ama and I said together.

"Want to go get something to eat?" Ama asked us, but Shiba-san said, "No, it's too early for me," and we left on our own. On the way home I turned my neck around as far as it would go and looked down at my back. I could see the parts of the Kirin and dragon that weren't covered by the dress and I could feel Ama looking at me with what appeared to be mixed feelings.

"What is it?" I asked with my eyes, but he just looked away and frowned. That kind of silent treatment really makes me angry, so I quickened my pace to keep a half step in front of him. Seeing what I was doing right away, he grabbed my hand and pulled himself along to catch up with me, still wearing the same look on his face.

"Lui, why did you wear a dress there? I mean, you got naked down to your panties to have the tattoo done anyway, right?"

"I just thought a dress would be more comfortable than a T-shirt afterward."

With his head still down and without saying anything, he just strengthened his grip on my hand. Then when we came to a stop at a red light, he finally looked up at me.

"Am I pathetic?" he asked.

I felt something close to sympathy for him. It always broke my heart to see a guy give himself to someone so completely.

"A little," I answered.

He smiled awkwardly. Then when I returned it with a small smile of my own, he pulled me into a tight embrace—drawing glances from strangers passing by.

"Do you not like pathetic guys?"

"Not much."

He strengthened his grip on me, and I found it a little hard to breathe.

"I'm sorry. But as I'm sure you know, I love you, Lui."

When he finally let go, I saw his eyes were a little red, making him look like a junkie, so I rubbed his head and he laughed like a stupid little kid.

That night I drank until I dropped—literally. Ama seemed to enjoy looking after me, though, so it wasn't a problem. It had already been a month since the Shinjuku incident, and Ama was still by my side. I told myself that everything was all right; that everything was going to be fine. I had my tongue stud, and I was looking forward to when my tattoo would be done and my forked tongue complete.

I wondered if changing myself like this could be considered an insult to God, or an act of pure ego. I thought of how my life had no real possessions, no emotional ties, no hatred. And it made me feel that my tattoo, my forked tongue, my future, were all empty of meaning as well.

Four months after we'd first decided on the design, my tattoo was complete. It had taken just four sessions and Shiba-san had fucked me at the end of each one, but on the day of the fourth and final session he uncharacteristically wiped the cum off my stomach with a tissue.

"Perhaps I should quit doing tattoos," he said, staring into space as he spoke. I had no reason to stop him, so I said nothing and simply lit a cigarette.

"I'm thinking of sticking with one girl. You know, like Ama," he said.

"That have anything to do with quitting doing tattoos?"

"Maybe. I've been thinking I maybe need to make a new start in life. After all, now I've finished the greatest Kirin ever, I'd be able to quit without any regrets," he said, rubbing his head. Then he let out a deep sigh and said, "As if I could, though. Forget I even said that. I'm just always thinking about changing jobs."

Shiba-san still had his top off and the Kirin glared at me from where it sat, perched on his arm like a king reigning over its land.

In time, the dragon and the Kirin both shed their scabs, completing their transformation to be a part of my body. Now, they were really my possessions—a word I liked to use when I thought of them—but one that could also become devalued after the initial excitement of a new thing wore off. I mean one day, you've got a wonderful new skirt, for example, that makes you feel great. But in just a short time, that skirt's become just another item in your wardrobe. I was kind of fickle like that, I guess, often relegating a thing to the back of the closet after only wearing it two, maybe three times. I guess I tend to see marriage in a similar way too. Just a situation where two people are trying to possess each other. Or even if you're not married, guys still tend to push the same kind of thing, becoming gradually more and more domineering the longer you stay with them. It's what's known as the "why feed a fish if it's already in your net" mentality, but when a fish runs out of food, it has one of two choices: to escape or die. Still the struggle to possess seems to be the unifying element in all relationships. Maybe it appeals to the masochist and sadist in every one of us. As for me, however, no matter what else, I knew I'd always possess a beautiful dragon and a Kirin right there on my back. They'd never betray me, and without eyes they'd never fly away. They'd always, always be there.

The hole in my tongue, which could only hold a 10g before the tattooing began, had now grown to accommodate a 6g. And every time I stretched it further it hurt so much I kept thinking that this was as big as it was ever going to get. On every day where I'd moved up to a bigger stud, I found I couldn't even taste anything for the rest of the day. The constant pain also made me me irritable and made me wish that everybody would just die.

And in my typical selfishness, I took all my frustrations out on Ama. That's me, though, just simple. With all the intelligence and values of a monkey.

The world outside the window was cold and gray. It was the second week in December, and you could smell the dryness of the air the moment you stepped outside the front door. Being a freeter, someone who just picks up temp jobs here and there, it really didn't make any difference to me what day of the week it was. It was more than a month since my tattoo had been completed, but somehow I still felt as if it had sapped all the energy out of me. I told myself that it was probably just the cold weather and willed the days to pass as quickly as possible. Not that it would even make a difference anyway. After all, there's no point in me waiting for a solution when I don't even have a problem in the first place. Life just seemed so empty, that's all. I'd just wake up in the morning, see Ama off, then go back to sleep again pretty much every day. Once in a while, I'd go out and do a little work, maybe have sex with Shiba-san or meet up with friends, but no matter what I did, I always ended up feeling low. When Ama came home at night, we would go out for dinner, sharing a plate of this and a plate of that interspersed with drinks. Then we'd go back home and carry on with the drinking. I wondered if I was turning into an alcoholic. Ama was worried about me too. He'd keep fussing over me and do his best to cheer me up by talking excitedly about this and that. Then when that wouldn't work, he'd just burst into tears, crying "Why? Why?" at me, and going on about how angry and hurt he felt.

Seeing him like that made me want to respond to his feelings, but whenever a tiny seed of hope took root in me and began to grow, it was always crushed by a heavy downpour of self-loathing. Simply put, there was just no light. My life and future were pitch black, and I couldn't see anything at the end of the tunnel. It's not as if I'd been expecting great things for myself before that, it's just that now I could clearly imagine myself turning up dead in a gutter somewhere and I didn't even really have the energy to laugh it off. At least before I met Ama, I'd always been prepared to sell my body if it came down to that. But now I just couldn't bring myself to do anything other than sleep and eat. In fact, I thought I'd rather die than go with stinking middle-aged men. I wondered which would be better—to work as a prostitute to live, or to die rather than work as one? I'd say the latter answer would be the one chosen by the healthy mind, but then again, there's not really anything healthy about being dead. Anyway, they do say that women who are sexually active tend to have a better complexion. Not that I cared if I was healthy or not.

On the day I stretched my tongue hole to a 4g, blood oozed out of it pretty freely and I couldn't bring myself to eat, so I just drank beer. Ama said I was rushing my tongue, but I didn't care—I was in a hurry. Of course, it wasn't as if I was up against the clock or suffering from something terminal; it's just that I was getting this strong feeling that time was running out. Maybe there are just some times in life when things need to be rushed.

"Do you ever feel that you want to die?" Ama asked out of the blue one night after we had come home from dinner and drinks.

"All the time," I said.

He just stared emptily at the beer in his glass for a

while, then let out a sigh and said, "I won't let anybody kill you. Not even yourself. If you decide to take your own life, you have to let me do it. I wouldn't be able to stand anybody but myself determining your fate."

Ama's words reminded me of Shiba-san. I wondered which one of them I would ask to do the deed when the temptation finally became too much. Which one would do the best job of it? That turned my thoughts to Desire, and I decided I'd go there the next day. For some reason, as soon as I decided on that, an inkling of a will to live returned to me.

After seeing Ama off to work around noon, I put on some makeup and was just about to call Shiba-san, when he called me, as if he'd read my mind or something.

"Hi?"

"It's me. Can you talk?"

"Sure. I was just thinking of coming over to your place today. Is something the matter?"

"Yeah, well, it's about Ama."

"What is it?"

"Do you know if he was involved in some kind of trouble sometime in July?"

I felt my chest tighten at Shiba-san's words, and the image of Ama repeatedly punching the guy came to my mind.

"I don't know . . . Why do you ask?"

"The police just came by and asked me to show them my list of tattoo clients. They wanted to know who had gotten dragon tattoos. I only keep a list of first-time customers, and Ama's name wasn't on it, so I guess there's nothing to worry about. But still . . ."

"It's not him they were looking for. He's been with me the whole time."

"I'm sure he has. Sorry. It's just they said the guy had red hair. And you know Ama had red hair then, so I just kind of wondered."

"I see," I said and inhaled deeply. My heart was beating so hard it was shaking my entire body, and I had to concentrate on my hand to make sure I didn't drop the phone. I wondered if I should confide in Shiba-san. It would take a huge weight off my mind and I would like to know his thoughts on it, but would it really be the

85

right thing to do? He might tell Ama. And I didn't know what Ama would do if he found out that I had seen the article in the paper. Would he turn himself in? Would he skip town? He was normally so easy to understand and we spent so much time together, but I suddenly felt an uneasy distance when I realized I had absolutely no idea how he would react. What does go through someone's mind when they kill someone anyway? Do they think about the future? The people they care about? Their life all the way up to that moment? And how could I even begin to guess? I was a person who could see no future for myself; a person who cared about no one. I couldn't even understand my own life, which was little more than a pastiche of drunken moments. All I knew was that over the weeks and over the months, I had come to have feelings for Ama.

"Lui, don't worry about it. So you coming over today?"

"Actually . . . I think I'll stay home today. Maybe another time."

"Come over. Please. I want to talk to you."

"I don't know. I'll see how I feel."

I put down the phone, paced the room a little and tried to compose my thoughts. Unfortunately, however, my thoughts had other plans, so I got frustrated and decided on a drink. I opened a bottle of sake that Ama and I were planning to drink together, put it to my lips, and swallowed it down direct. It tasted even better than I'd expected, and it was going down really well too. I could feel it filling up my otherwise empty stomach. I drank the entire bottle, then I finished off my makeup and walked out the door.

"Good afternoon."

"Good afternoon? Since when have we been so formal?" said Shiba-san with a frown as he turned to see me standing by the door.

"Life got you down?" he asked with a wry smile. I smiled back weakly and walked up to the counter. The strong perfume of an incense stick smoldering on the counter hit my nose and made me want to throw up immediately.

"I'm not kidding. Something's wrong with you."

"Like what?"

"When did I see you last?"

"About two weeks ago?"

"And how much weight have you lost since then?"

"I don't know. Ama doesn't have any scales."

"You're sickly thin. Sickly thin and totally pale. And you stink of alcohol."

I looked at my reflection in the glass showcase. It was true. I looked like a crane fly. I couldn't believe how grotesque I looked. I guess this is what happens when you lose the will to live. I remembered how I had been basically living on alcohol and bar food. In fact, I couldn't recall the last time I'd had a proper meal. At the time, though, I thought this seemed really funny and I couldn't help myself from laughing out loud.

"Isn't Ama feeding you properly?"

"Ama? He's always nagging me to eat more, but I'm happy just drinking."

"If you keep this up, you'll starve. Then how are you going to kill yourself?"

"I'm not going to kill myself," I said, and walked past Shiba-san into the back room.

"I'll go buy something. What will you eat?"

"Get me some beers."

"I've got beers in the fridge. Anything else?"

"Shiba-san, have you ever killed anyone?"

Shiba-san stared at me for a second, sending a sharp

pain shooting through my body. "Well . . ." He left a long pause that felt like forever. "Yes," he said, then came closer and stroked my hair.

I don't know why, but tears welled up in my eyes and began streaming down my face.

"How did it feel?" I asked, my voice shivering with tears.

"It felt good," he replied, as if all I'd asked was, *How was your bath?*

I was obviously asking the wrong person.

"Good, huh?" I said, wishing I hadn't started crying.

"Take off your clothes."

"I thought you were going shopping."

"Your crying face gave me a hard-on."

I took off all my clothes except my underwear and reached out to Shiba-san, who was wearing a white shirt and gray pants. He unbuckled his belt, then picked me up and placed me on the bed. My crotch responded to his cold stare—like a weird sexual version of one of Pavlov's dogs.

Within seconds it felt like his fingers and penis were everywhere. Poking me, prodding me, making me gasp and grimace with pain and with pleasure. I felt as if his fingers were getting rougher each and every time we had

89

sex. It was probably a sign of his passion, I thought, but if he continued like this, then one day he would end up killing me.

When we'd finished, I stayed on the bed, and Shiba-san got up to get his cigarettes.

He sat down next to me, lit a cigarette, and said, "Why don't you marry me?"

"Is that what you wanted to talk about?"

"Yeah. Ama is too much for you to handle. And you're too much for him. You guys just aren't compatible."

"And me and you are?"

"Nah. That's a whole different question. I just kind of want to get married." He said it in a real nonchalant manner, but it was still a strange thing to say. *I just kind of want to get married?* Proposals surely don't come any less heartfelt than that. Without waiting for my response, Shiba-san stood up and put on his clothes. Then he walked over to the desk and took something metallic out of the drawer.

"I went ahead and made you a ring anyway," he said, and handed me a huge ring that covered my entire finger from the knuckle right down to the nail. It even had joints so you could move your finger, and although the design couldn't be any more punk, it was pretty well made. I slipped the ring onto my index finger.

"You made this?"

"Yeah, it's one of my hobbies. Though I guess it's not exactly your kind of thing."

"Wow. Well, it's uh . . . chunky," I said, and laughed, which brought a grin to Shiba-san's face. "Thank you," I said, and gave him a kiss. Shiba-san shrugged off the kiss and said that he was going to pop over to the store.

After Shiba-san stepped out to the store, I thought about what he had said about Ama and me not being compatible with each other. What exactly did it mean to be compatible anyway? Was it even possible for two people to be completely compatible with each other?

I found myself thinking about the possibility of marriage, though the whole idea seemed unrealistic. In fact everything seemed pretty distant to me. The thoughts in my head. The scene in front of my eyes. The cigarette I was holding between my middle and index fingers. It was as if I was looking down at myself from some faraway place. There was nothing for me to believe and nothing for me to feel. In fact the only feeling with the power to kick me back to life was the feeling of acute pain.

Shiba-san came back from the convenience store with some food.

"Here, eat some of this. At least a few bites."

Shiba-san placed a serving of pork cutlet on rice and beef on rice in front of me.

"Which one do you want?"

"I don't want either, thanks. Can I have a beer?"

I got to my feet before Shiba-san could answer and took out a beer from the fridge. Then I sat down on a pipe chair next to the desk and tipped it down my throat. Shiba-san looked at me as if to say, *Hopeless.*

"Okay, be like that. See if I care. Just let me know if you want to get married, okay?"

"Will do!" I said cheerfully, and downed the rest of my beer.

I headed home before it got dark. Outside, a cold wind was blowing. I wondered how much longer I could live, and I had a sense that it wouldn't be long. Once I got back to Ama's place, I put in a 2g tongue stud. Blood started to run out straight away and the pain was so bad it brought tears to my eyes. I didn't know why I was doing this. I knew that Ama would be angry with me when he got back, and drank another beer to dull the pain while I waited for him.

Ama never came home that night. Something must have happened, that was pretty much for sure. After all, ever since we'd been living together there'd never been a single instance of him not coming home. He was extremely conscientious and always came back to the room where I waited. That's the way it always was with us, and we'd come to rely on things being exactly that way. Even if he was going to be just a little bit later coming back from work, he always phoned to tell me.

Not once had he failed to come home. I called his mobile phone, but it just went straight to the voice mail without ringing even once. I tried again and again, but the result was always the same. That night I didn't sleep at all, and by the morning I had bags under my eyes. I didn't know what to do and I started to get angry at Ama for leaving me all alone. I wondered what he was thinking. What he was doing. And somewhere inside me I felt an awful feeling that something in my life was coming quietly to an end.

"Ama." My pathetic voice echoed through the room—

a room without Ama. I'd put in a 2g tongue stud and I wanted to tell him. I wanted him to smile and be happy for me. To tell me he was glad that I was one step closer to a forked tongue. To get pissed off at me for drinking all the sake on my own.

Eventually, I managed to get myself to stop thinking. Then I braced myself, walked to the door and strode out with renewed determination.

"You don't have to be family to report a missing person, do you?" I asked at the police box.

"No, you don't."

I felt I could have punched the policeman for his blasé attitude.

"Make sure to bring a photo of the guy when you do."

I walked off without answering, moving at a fast pace but no real direction. Then the severity of the situation suddenly hit me.

"I don't know Ama's name . . . ," I muttered to myself.

Without a name I couldn't even report him missing.

When I saw Shiba-san, he looked into my angry face as if there was something he wanted to say.

"What's Ama's name?" I asked.

"Huh? What are you on about?"

"Ama didn't come home. I need to report him missing."

"What, you don't even know his name?"

"No."

"But you two live together."

"I know," I said, tears welling up in my eyes.

"Don't cry. You must have seen his name outside the front door or on letters and stuff," said Shiba-san, looking into my eyes with a look of total surprise, maybe at my sudden tears.

"Ama doesn't have his name up outside the door, and the postbox is so full of leaflets that I never bothered opening it."

"He went to work as usual yesterday, right? So he didn't come back last night?"

"No. He hasn't been back since he went to work yesterday."

"Why are you getting so worked up about it? It's only one night. I'm sure everything is fine. Don't panic just because he didn't come home for a night. He's not a kid, you know."

His inability to grasp the situation was seriously starting to irritate me.

"All this time that we've been living together, Ama has never stayed out without telling me. He even calls me if he's going to be half an hour late."

Shiba-san looked down at the counter and said nothing. Then he looked up at me and muttered, "But still . . ."

Maybe I shouldn't have been so worried, and I started to wonder if Shiba-san was right. That there was nothing to worry about. It was only one night, as he said. But no, I had to look for Ama. That's when I decided to play my trump card.

"Ama might have killed someone."

"You mean the pimp guy in Shinjuku the police were talking about?"

"It was my fault. If I'd just ignored that guy, Ama never would have beat him up. I didn't think he would die. So when I saw the newspaper article, I didn't think it could be the same person. I was sure it was someone else. I didn't think that it could have been about Ama . . ."

"If you report him missing, Ama might get caught by the police. If he found out the police were looking for him and he's on the run, he might have a better chance of getting away if we pretend we don't know anything about him."

"But I'm worried about him. It hurts not to know where he is, what he's doing and what he's thinking. I know that Ama wouldn't try to run away on his own. He would have said something to me. He would have wanted to take me with him."

"Okay then. Let's go."

Shiba-san closed the store and we headed to the police station. Shiba-san filed a missing person's report and handed the policeman a photograph of Ama with his top off.

"I didn't know you had his photograph," I said.

"Huh? Oh, yeah, I took it when I did his dragon."

"Mr. Kazunori Amada . . . ," said the policeman, looking at the form. And that was the first time I'd ever heard Ama's real name. It wasn't Amadeus after all, I thought. I told myself I'd give him a hard time about that as soon as I could see him again, and the very thought

97

brought tears to my eyes. At first, just a little. Then in floods that I couldn't stop. I felt completely calm, and yet the tears kept pouring out.

"You okay?" asked Shiba-san, stroking my hair. But I couldn't stop myself crying, and I walked to the entrance of the police station and flopped down on a bench. Why? Why did he disappear so suddenly? I bent over and cried out loud.

A little while later Shiba-san came over, having finished all the paperwork. My vision was still blurry, and still I couldn't stop my tears. I felt like a child as I wiped them on my coat sleeve.

Shiba-san and I took a taxi back to Ama's place.

"Ama?" I called out from the door, but there was no response. Shiba-san stroked my head from behind me, and wiped my tears when they came pouring out again. Once inside, I sat on the wooden floor, and cried again. Shiba-san sat on the bed and watched me as I kept on crying. "Why? Why!" I screamed, and punched the floor. The ring Shiba-san had given me made a dull thud on the wood of the floor, and for some reason the sound brought more tears to my eyes. Why? Why did he leave me all alone? Once my tears stopped, I could feel the anger building inside me. I clenched my teeth, until my jaw began to hurt and I heard something crack in the back of my mouth. I felt around my mouth with my tongue and found I'd chipped a tooth with a cavity. I crushed the splinter between my teeth and swallowed it. *Become a part of me*, I thought. *Become my flesh and blood.* Because I wanted everything to become a part of me. Because I so wanted Ama to melt into me. He loved me and I would rather have him become one with me than disappear from my life. Then I'd never have to be away from him ever again. He said I was important to him. So why did he leave me? How could he leave me?

The silence of the room was shattered with a wail of pain coming from deep within me. I opened the jewelry box I shared with Ama and took out a tongue stud. I'd stretched the hole to a 2g only yesterday, and there was no way it would stretch further. But I took out a short square stud—the 0g milestone—and saw the color drain from Shiba-san's face as he suddenly understood what I was going to do.

"Is that a 0? You were wearing a 4 only yesterday."

I didn't turn around to acknowledge Shiba-san's words. Instead I faced the mirror, took out the 2g stud and began to force in the 0g stud. When it was halfway in, a sharp pain shot through me, but instead of stopping, I pushed the stud all the way in. Shiba-san shot his hand out, to try to take it off me, but it was already too late. The stud was embedded firmly in my tongue.

"What the hell are you doing?"

Shiba-san opened my mouth and looked into it with a frown on his face.

"Stick out your tongue."

I did as I was told, and blood trickled down my tongue and dripped onto the floor, along with the tears that were rolling off my cheeks.

"Take it out."

When I shook my head, his face fell.

"I told you not to overdo it," he said, and held me tight in his arms.

It was the first time he'd ever held me. Not knowing what to do, I just sat there in his arms, swallowing the blood that was streaming out of my tongue.

"I'm going to split it after I put in a 00g," I said.

My words were slurred and sloppy, like Ama's smile.

"Okay. Okay."

I realized my tears had stopped. I wondered what Ama would say when he saw the 0g stud in my tongue. I was sure he would smile and be happy for me. He would say "Not long to go now."

I drank beer and cried and cried and waited for Ama. Shiba-san was looking at me the entire time but didn't say anything. Eventually night came. The room grew cold and I began to shiver. Without saying anything, Shiba-san turned on the heater and put a blanket over my shoulder as I sat there without moving. My tongue had stopped bleeding, but the tears continued to come and go. My feelings moved back and forth between sadness and anger. Eventually the clock struck seven—the time Ama usually came home from work. I looked up at the clock every ten seconds and kept opening and shutting my cell phone. I called Ama's phone a few times, but all I got each time was the voice mail.

"You know what store Ama works at?"

"You don't?" said Shiba-san, looking surprised.

He was right. Ama and I knew nothing about each other.

"No, I don't."

"It's a secondhand clothing store. You guys really don't know anything about each other, do you? So you haven't contacted them yet?"

"No."

Shiba-san flipped open his mobile and clicked through his address book.

"It's me. I'm calling about Ama . . . Yeah. Just didn't come into work, huh? . . . Yeah. He hasn't come home . . . Don't know yet . . . Yeah. I'll contact you as soon as I know something."

It was obvious that nobody at the store knew anything. Shiba-san hung up and sighed.

"The guy said that he left work at the usual time yesterday, but he didn't come in today. Didn't call in sick or anything. The guy was pissed off. Said he tried calling Ama's cell but couldn't get through. I know the owner of the store. Actually, he hired Ama as a favor to me."

I knew nothing about Ama. Until yesterday, I'd thought that all I needed to know about Ama was what I saw with my own eyes. But now I realized I was blind because that's all I looked for. Why hadn't I asked his name or asked about his family?

"Doesn't Ama have any family?"

"I'm not sure. I think he has at least one parent. I think I remember him talking about his dad."

"Right," I muttered and once again began to cry.

"Let's go get something to eat. I'm starving."

As soon as Shiba-san said that, I started to cry again. It reminded me of how I would fill myself up on beer, and how Ama would always go on about how he was starving then drag me out to get something to eat.

"I'll stay here. But you should go, Shiba-san."

Shiba-san said nothing. He just walked over to the kitchen and began rummaging through the contents of the fridge. "All you've got is alcohol," he said, then took out a pack of salted squid. At that moment, Shiba-san's phone rang.

"It's ringing," I said. My voice much louder than I'd expected. My heart beat so hard I felt sick. I put a hand against my chest, picked up the phone with the other hand, and threw it to Shiba-san. He caught it and answered it.

"Hello? . . . Yes . . . Ah, yes. I understand. We'll head over straightaway."

When Shiba-san got off the phone, he put a firm hand on my shoulder and stared into my eyes.

103

"They found a body in Yokosuka. It might not be Ama, but the body has a dragon tattoo on it. They want us to go over to the morgue to identify the body."

"Right."

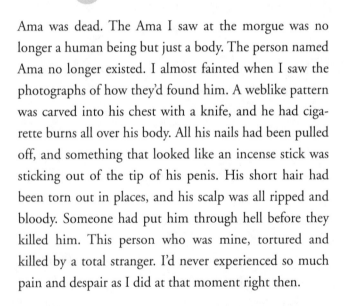

Ama was dead. The Ama I saw at the morgue was no longer a human being but just a body. The person named Ama no longer existed. I almost fainted when I saw the photographs of how they'd found him. A weblike pattern was carved into his chest with a knife, and he had cigarette burns all over his body. All his nails had been pulled off, and something that looked like an incense stick was sticking out of the tip of his penis. His short hair had been torn out in places, and his scalp was all ripped and bloody. Someone had put him through hell before they killed him. This person who was mine, tortured and killed by a total stranger. I'd never experienced so much pain and despair as I did at that moment right then.

Ama's body was taken away for an autopsy—to be cut up even more—and my tired mind couldn't even feel any anger. My last words to Ama had been "Take care!" I had shouted them to him without even turning around as my mind had been on my plans to visit Shiba-san. Shiba-san lent me his hand each time I staggered, and he caught me when I collapsed to my knees at the mortuary.

I had been right. There was no light in my future.

"Pull yourself together, Lui."

"I can't."

"At least eat something."

"I can't."

"Then at least try to get some sleep."

"Can't."

After they found Ama's body, I had gone to stay with Shiba-san for a while, and we had this same conversation many times.

Then he'd tut and say, "Can't even have a normal conversation."

The autopsy revealed that Ama had been strangled, but he'd still been alive through all the horrific mutilation.

I didn't give a shit about those kinds of details, though. I just wanted them to find out who'd done it. Surely there must be clues. At first I could only imagine that it was friends of the guy from that night in Shinjuku, but after I saw the body I somehow changed my mind. It just seemed too extreme, not like the work of some low-level mob guy at all. No gangster would risk leaving the evidence of so many cigarette burns or push an incense stick up his penis.

Whoever it was, I wished they'd thrown the body into Tokyo Bay. At least that way it might never have been found and I could have gone on believing that he was still alive somewhere.

There was no doubt that Ama had killed the guy. But now that both the victim and perpetrator were dead, the incident had been rendered meaningless.

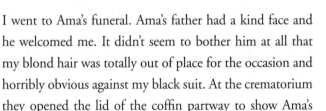

I went to Ama's funeral. Ama's father had a kind face and he welcomed me. It didn't seem to bother him at all that my blond hair was totally out of place for the occasion and horribly obvious against my black suit. At the crematorium they opened the lid of the coffin partway to show Ama's face, but I couldn't look in. I didn't want to say goodbye. I wanted to believe that the Ama I had seen at the morgue was still alive, and that the person inside the coffin was someone else. All I could do was escape from reality, but every time I tried to escape from the pain, that same pain told me that I had probably been falling in love with him.

"When will the murderer be caught?" I asked the police after the funeral.

"We are doing what we can."

"And what are you doing exactly?"

"Lui, stop it," said Shiba-san, holding me back. What were they doing at the funeral when they couldn't even catch the murderer? I couldn't hold back my anger.

"What? You think I'm out of line? That I'm being out of place by telling you to do your job? You're just going to let it go, though, aren't you? You think you can cut corners in your work because Ama killed someone. You can all go to hell. Make everyone happy."

"That's enough, Lui. You're being hysterical."

I collapsed onto the ground and broke down in tears. Screw you. Go to hell, you fuckers. I wish I had a greater vocabulary to fully express the extent of my pain and hatred. But I don't. I'm just pathetic. That's all I am.

Five days had passed since Ama died, but still they hadn't found the killer. During that time I hadn't left the house once since coming out of the hospital that Shiba-san had taken me to, so Shiba-san asked me to come work with him at the store. Sometimes he would try to have sex with me, but he couldn't manage it, as I would remain expressionless even when he strangled me. I wanted him to just go ahead and kill me. If I'd actually told him so, he probably would have done it gladly. But I never did. I didn't know if that was because it was too much trouble, because I still had the desire to live, or because I wanted to believe that Ama was still alive. In fact, the only thing I did know was that I *was* still alive. I was living a boring existence without Ama. A monotonous, sexless life. And to make matters worse, I'd also stopped eating altogether and had gone from 42 kilograms to only 34 kilograms in just six months. I felt there was no point in eating when all we do is just shit it out anyway. Though I did actually still need to go to the bathroom, even though I was consuming nothing but alcohol. That's due to what they call fecal impaction, apparently, where there's pretty much always a kind of reserve of shit in your system. That's what the doctor told me anyway. He also told me very kindly that I'd die if I kept on losing weight the way I had been. He recommended that I stay at the hospital, but Shiba-san declined. I couldn't understand why he bothered to take care of a girl he couldn't even fuck.

"Lui, can you organize the stuff on this rack."

I did as I was told and picked up some bags of earrings I had just priced and headed toward the rack. Shiba-san was cleaning the store from corner to corner. Trying to blow the cobwebs away and start anew, I thought. It reminded me that the year was coming to an end. That the weather was getting colder. That Christmas was just around the corner. In fact, come to think of it, maybe Shiba-san was just following the New Year cleaning tradition.

"Shiba-san."

"Don't you think it's about time you dropped the 'san'?"

I wondered if that meant he thought we were an item.

"My name's Kizuki Shibata."

109

I'd already known this, as I'd seen the nameplate outside his apartment.

"Sounds like a girl's name, doesn't it, 'Kizuki.' I don't know why, but everyone calls me Shiba."

"What should I call you?"

"Kizuki is fine."

Ama and I had never had a conversation like this. A conversation like those of normal couples. Perhaps that was why I had so many regrets and I couldn't let him go. I regretted not having talked about normal things with him; about family, the past, names, ages, and so on. At the funeral, I learned for the first time that he was eighteen years old. I only found out that I'd been going out with a guy younger than me for the first time in my life after he'd died. I was nineteen, so that made me a year older than him. It was something normal couples would have talked about the first day they met.

"Kizuki."

It felt strange calling him that, but I decided I would anyway.

"What is it?"

"This rack's already full. I can't put any more on it."

"Just put them anywhere. Put them on the next rack over if you like. Or just stuff them in there."

I pushed the bags of earrings into the rack. It was a really tight squeeze but the bags somehow fit in. Watching the earrings made me think of Ama. After he'd died, I couldn't even be bothered to stretch my tongue hole any further, even though the pain had subsided a while ago. Perhaps my tongue hole had no meaning now there wasn't anyone to praise me for it. Perhaps I'd been trying to get a forked tongue just to share the same feeling with Ama. If I stretched the hole by one more gauge, I would reach 00g. That was the point where Ama had split his tongue. But my strong desire had suddenly fizzled out just a step away from the finish line. After all, what was the point of a forked tongue now I had lost Ama and all interest? I returned to the counter, sat down on a pipe chair, and stared into space. I didn't feel like doing anything.

"Lui, mind if I ask you what your name is?"

"You want to know?"

"That's why I'm asking you."

"It's Lui for Louis Vuitton."

"No, your real name."

"Lui Nakazawa."

"So Lui is your real name. How about family? Do you have any parents?"

"People always assume I'm an orphan, but yes, I do have parents. They live in Saitama."

"Really. I didn't expect that. I guess I'll have to go introduce myself sometime."

I wondered why people always took me for an orphan. In reality, both my parents were alive, and there was no trouble in our family. Shiba-san carried on dusting the racks, and I just spent the day watching him.

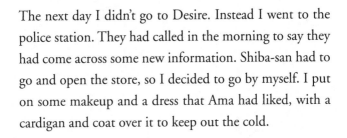

The next day I didn't go to Desire. Instead I went to the police station. They had called in the morning to say they had come across some new information. Shiba-san had to go and open the store, so I decided to go by myself. I put on some makeup and a dress that Ama had liked, with a cardigan and coat over it to keep out the cold.

"All the cigarette burns were from Marlboro Menthols," said the policeman, "and we're having the saliva analyzed. Also, the incense stick that was inserted into his penis. It's a brand called Ecstasy. Imported from the U.S. Musk."

So fucking what? What good is that information to anyone, I thought, the anger inside me welling up even more. Ama, Shiba-san, Maki, me; we all smoked Marlboro Menthols. It didn't mean anything.

"You can buy incense anywhere," I said abruptly.

"Well, yes. But this one is only sold in the Kanto region. There's um . . . something else we wanted to ask you today too."

I noticed a nervous flicker in his face.

"Do you know if Mr. Amada had any bisexual tendencies?"

That was it. My anger hit the roof. I was well aware he meant no offense, but I still wanted to drill the ring on my index finger—the one Shiba-san had given me—right into his face.

"Why do you ask? Was Ama raped?"

"The autopsy did indicate that, yes."

I took a deep breath and traced back my memory. Ama didn't have any abnormal sexual tendencies. We had sex almost every day, but it was straightforward to the point where I was starting to lose interest in it. He couldn't have been bisexual. It made me sick to even think he'd been raped by another guy.

"No, he wasn't bisexual. I can vouch for that."

113

On my way out I gave every policeman I passed a lingering look filled with hatred. I headed to Desire to tell Shiba-san about the lack of progress in the investigation. I didn't want to believe that Ama had been raped. But at the same time, I knew that there was no way he would have let someone do that to him. Even if he was bisexual, I was sure that he would have been the butch, not the femme, in the relationship.

I opened the front door of Desire and smiled weakly at Shiba-san who was sitting behind the counter smoking. I couldn't tell him what had really happened to Ama. I didn't want his image to be tainted in anyone else's mind.

"They've found nothing whatsoever."

Shiba-san smiled weakly, as if imitating me, and said, "Right."

Shiba-san had become kind to me ever since Ama's death. He still had a savage tongue, but more and more I could feel thoughtfulness and kindness in his expressions and actions. He walked me to the back room, and went back to the store once he'd laid me down on the bed. I stayed there for a while, but decided I wouldn't be able to fall asleep sober, so I got up and opened the fridge. I opened a cheap bottle of red wine and drank it straight from the bottle. Then I felt hungry for the first time in a very long while, so I took a piece of bread from the fridge, broke off a section, and took a bite out of it. The smell of yeast made me nauseous, however, so I put it back in the fridge and slammed the door shut. Then I sat on the desk chair with the bottle of wine in one hand and took my makeup bag out of my bag, and gazed at the teeth Ama had called the "symbol of his love." I took them out and rolled them around on the palm of my hand. I wondered what they could possibly mean now that he was gone. Why was I even looking at them? I found myself looking at the teeth more often since Ama had disappeared from my life. Every time I put them back in my bag, I felt overwhelmed with a sense of hopelessness. Would the day I stopped looking at the teeth be the day that I got Ama out of my mind? Then, as I put them back in my makeup bag once again, something caught my eye. I could see a thin paper package sticking out of the half-open desk drawer, and in just a split second I assumed the very worst. I reached over and took the package out of the drawer. Musk Ecstasy incense.

Immediately I got up out of the chair.

"I'm going shopping."

"Where to?" asked Shiba-san, looking surprised, but I

headed straight out the door without answering or turning back, my feet carrying me full speed in the direction of the store.

When I returned to Desire, out of breath, Shiba-san stroked my head with a look of concern.

"Where did you go, Lui? You had me worried."

"I went to buy some incense. I don't like the smell of musk."

I fetched the pack of incense from the desk, bunched up all the incense sticks inside the pack, and split them all in half before throwing them into the trash can.

"I got coconut instead," I said, lighting an incense stick.

"Is something the matter, Lui?"

"No. Nothing's the matter. By the way, Kizuki, I think you should grow your hair. I like long hair on guys."

Shiba-san laughed at my suggestion. If this was before, he would have probably glared at me and told me to shut up and mind my own business, but he said, "Why not? Guess I might give long hair a try for a change."

That night I went home with Shiba-san and managed to eat a little dinner. It made me want to puke, but Shiba-san looked really glad to see me eating, so I held it down.

I then got into bed with him and lay next to him until he fell asleep, all the time replaying sickening scenes of him strangling Ama as he raped him. I imagined a whole range of different, sickening things, like Ama laughing through it all, or Shiba-san crying. If Shiba-san really was the murderer, he must have choked Ama so much harder than he ever choked me. Once I was sure he was sound asleep, I went into the living room, cracked open a beer, and stared at Ama's love token. Then I rummaged through the shelves by the front door until I found a hammer. I wrapped the two teeth first in a plastic bag and then in a towel, then I smashed them into tiny pieces with the hammer. The dull thudding of the hammer made my heart shiver. Next I put all the bits and pow-dered remains in my mouth and washed them down with beer, which was the only thing I tasted. Then that was that. That was all it took for Ama's token of love to be-come a part of me forever.

The next day I went to Desire with Shiba-san and opened up the store with him. I ate a little piece, though I do mean a little piece, of bread he'd bought for me. It was enough, however, to put a look of satisfaction on his face.

"Kizuki, I have a favor to ask you."

"What is it?"

I took off my dress and lay down on the bed.

"You sure?"

I nodded my head. He picked up that tool—the one that looked like a ballpoint pen—and prepared to paint eyes for my dragon and my Kirin; to give them the gift of life. "Coming in now." Together with Shiba-san's words, a sharp pain shot through my back. I didn't know exactly why I'd decided to get a tattoo in the first place anymore, but I knew that this one had meaning for me. I wasn't just giving life to my dragon and my Kirin—I was giving it to myself.

"Aren't you worried they might fly away?" asked Shiba-san, as he pierced the skin of my back with his needle.

"They're free to do whatever they want." I laughed and stole a glance at Shiba-san's face. There and then, I knew he wouldn't be able to carry on violating me like he had. And I knew he would take care of me. That everything would be all right.

Even if Shiba-san had indeed raped and killed Ama, it was somehow still all right. And while I lay there engrossed in my thoughts, I saw a dragon and a Kirin open their eyes and stare at me in the mirror.

Just before closing time at Desire, I went back to Shiba-san's apartment. As soon as I got in the door, I walked to the mirror, took out my tongue stud, and started to tie dental floss in tight loops running though the hole and extending to the tip. When I pulled it tight, I felt only a dull pain and I could see I only had about 5mm of flesh left holding the tongue together. Naturally, it crossed my mind to just slice through the last part with a razor, but in the end I instead took a pair of eyebrow scissors and cut the dental floss off. It spun off my tongue like a spring uncoiling and the pain went away immediately. I looked at what was left in the mirror. Was this really what I had been chasing after? A useless, empty hole surrounded by raw flesh that glistened with spittle?

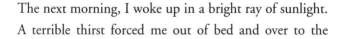

The next morning, I woke up in a bright ray of sunlight. A terrible thirst forced me out of bed and over to the

119

kitchen. I took a plastic bottle of ice-cold water from the fridge and drank it straight from the bottle, feeling it pass across and through my tongue, then flow smoothly downstream through my body, as if a river had formed inside me.

Shiba-san opened his eyes and slowly pushed himself up in bed. He looked at me staring into the mirror and rubbed his eyes.

"What are you doing?"

"There's a river inside me."

"What do you mean? I had a strange dream too."

"What kind of dream?"

"I used to be good friends with this guy who was into hip-hop and I was supposed to be meeting him, but I was late. Anyway, when I got there, he and his friends were mad at me, and they began rapping their anger. About five or six guys were standing around me, all rapping and singing their anger at me."

I kept my eyes on him as he slowly got out of bed, my mind still on the river that had grown inside me. I wondered if it would flow stronger if I were to stretch the hole in my tongue to a 00g. Then I turned to the sun, and I squinted into its unrelenting brightness.

ABOUT THE AUTHOR

Hitomi Kanehara was born in Tokyo on August 8, 1983. She was awarded the Subaru Prize for Literature in 2003 and the Akutagawa Prize in 2004 for her first novel, *Hebi ni piasu* (*Snakes and Earrings*). Her second novel, *Ash Baby*, was published in Japan in 2004.